MW01681383

Shadows of Loyalty

Jennifer Carr

JCarr WRITES

This is a work of fiction. Names, characters, organizations, places, events, and incidents are either products of the author's imagination or are used fictitiously. Any resemblance to actual persons, living or dead, is purely coincidental.

Published by JCarr Writes (jcarrwrites.com)

ISBN-13: 978-1969792007 (paperback)

ASIN: B0DX4LF4J5 (digital)

Part One

The Beginning

Chapter 1

Move-In Day

STEVEN

The sidewalks were alive with chaos—parents calling out final reminders, students hauling overflowing boxes, and the occasional honk of a car double-parked on the curb. The late-summer air was thick with humidity and nervous energy, a perfect match for the buzz running through me.

This was it. NYU. The start of everything.

I closed the trunk of my mom's car with a solid thunk and wiped my palms on my jeans, forcing a grin as I turned to her. She stood next to me, arms crossed, radiating concern. The "be careful" speech was coming; I could feel it.

"You'll call if you need anything?" she asked, bypassing the speech entirely in favor of direct emotional warfare.

"Mom," I said, exhaling a laugh, "I'll call. And text. And send postcards if I have to."

That earned a small smile, but the look in her eyes didn't soften. She pulled me into a tight hug, and I let her, even though my arms were full of my last box. "I'm proud of you," she whispered.

"I know. I'll be fine, I promise."

I watched as she climbed into the car and drove off, the taillights disappearing into the chaos of move-in day. For a second, I just stood there, letting the weight of this new chapter sink in. New York City felt like it was vibrating beneath my feet. There was so much to discover, so many stories waiting for me in every corner of the city. I adjusted the box in my arms and started toward Hayden Hall, a little bit of nervous excitement kicking in with every step.

The elevator was packed when I got there, a sea of frazzled parents and first-years squeezed in shoulder to shoulder. I opted for the stairs instead. I was halfway up when I saw her.

She was standing on the edge of a step, trying to wrestle an enormous suitcase up the stairs. Her long dark hair spilled over her face, and she shoved it back with a frustrated sigh, revealing a sharp but delicate profile. Something about her caught me off guard—the way she seemed out of sync with the chaos around her, like she was part of a different story altogether.

"Need a hand?" I asked before I could think twice.

She froze, glancing up at me. Her dark eyes locked on mine, and for a moment, I wondered if she was about to tell me to mind my own business. But then, after a heartbeat of hesitation, she gave me a small, almost reluctant smile.

"That'd be great," she said, stepping aside to let me take the handle.

I set my box down and grabbed the suitcase, letting out a low whistle as I hoisted it up. "What do you have in here, bricks?"

"Books," she replied, a hint of humor breaking through

her otherwise measured tone. "And maybe a few pairs of shoes."

"Must be a lot of books," I said, grinning as I hauled it up the stairs.

She stayed beside me, her steps light and deliberate. I couldn't quite read her—but that just made me more curious.

When we reached the fifth floor, I paused, catching my breath. "Which room?"

"502," she said, pulling a key from her pocket.

"Hey, same floor as me," I said, lifting the suitcase through the door as she held it open.

The room was mostly bare, just a couple of boxes stacked against the far wall. I set the suitcase down near the bed before turning for the door, only to see her watching me. She was still and quiet.

"Thanks for the help," she said, her voice warm but measured. "I'm Alessandra."

"Steven Porter," I replied, offering my hand.

She took it, her handshake firm and confident. "Nice to meet you."

I leaned against the doorframe, hoping she wouldn't mind a few more questions. Something about her made me want to stick around, like there was more to her story than she was letting on.

"So, what are you studying?" I asked.

"Business," she said. It sounded practiced, like she'd said it a hundred times before.

"You don't sound too excited about it," I said, testing the waters.

Her lips quirked into a small smile, but it didn't reach her eyes. "It's... practical."

"Is that what you want to study?"

Her eyes flicked up to mine before she gave a noncommittal shrug. "It's complicated."

Before I could press further, she tilted her head. "What about you?"

"Journalism," I said, the excitement bubbling back into my voice. "I've always wanted to dig into the stories no one else wants to touch, uncover the truth. Investigative stuff, mostly."

Her smile tightened slightly, and for the first time, she looked uneasy. "Sounds dangerous," she said softly.

"Yeah, but that's kind of the point," I said, grinning. "Nothing worth doing is safe, right?"

Her gaze lingered on me for a moment longer. Then she stepped back, the moment breaking.

"Maybe we could grab coffee sometime?" I asked, trying to sound casual.

She hesitated for a second, then gave a real smile—warm and unguarded. "Yeah, I'd like that."

We exchanged numbers, and I headed to retrieve the box I'd abandoned on the stairs then to my room feeling lighter than I had all day. As I unpacked, I kept glancing at my phone, trying not to overanalyze the way her smile had made me feel.

Finally, I caved and sent her a text:

Steven: Hey, it's Steven. Let me know when you're free for that coffee.

Her reply came almost instantly:

Alessandra: Looking forward to it.

I stared at the screen. She was already a mystery I wanted to solve.

Chapter 2

Don't Get Too Close

Alessandra

I closed the door behind Steven, the sound of the latch clicking into place louder than I expected. For a moment, I stood there, listening to the silence that settled in the room. He was gone, off to unpack and settle into his new life. I was left with mine. A life that was measured, already spoken for, with no room for distractions.

Steven Porter. I repeated his name in my head, filing it away. He struck me as genuine—the kind of person who'd offer to help without a second thought. That kind of kindness wasn't something I saw often. And it wasn't something I had the luxury of trusting.

I wandered to the window, pushing the thin curtain aside to glance down at the street below. The city was alive in a way that felt almost reckless—horns blaring, voices rising and falling, the pulse of a world that moved too fast for anyone to hold onto.

My world didn't move fast. It was slow by design. Controlled because it had to be.

Alessandra Navarra. The name echoed in my mind, a constant reminder of the rules I lived by. My father had made sure of that. I knew what was expected. I knew the cost of slipping up. There was no room for carelessness. No room for vulnerability.

I turned from the window. My phone sat on the bed, Steven's message blinking back at me:

Steven: *Hey, it's Steven. Let me know when you're free for that coffee.*

I'd replied almost before thinking:

Alessandra: *Looking forward to it.*

The words had gone out before I could second-guess them. Now they stared back at me, demanding an answer I couldn't give. Coffee was harmless. A polite response was expected.

But I knew better.

I sat on the edge of the bed, fingers tapping against the phone, trying to box the moment away before it grew into something more. This wasn't about Steven. It couldn't be. He seemed like a good guy—thoughtful, curious—but good guys didn't belong in my world.

I heard my father's voice in my head, cold and unyielding:

Distance is safety, Alessandra. Distance is survival.

My phone buzzed again. My stomach tightened, but the message was simple.

Steven: *Tomorrow after orientation? We can compare notes.*

I exhaled. He wasn't prying. He wasn't pushing. Not yet.

But journalists asked questions. That's what they did. Eventually, curiosity turned into investigation. I couldn't let it get that far.

Alessandra: *Sure, tomorrow works.*

The phone slipped from my hand. I leaned back and stared at the ceiling, trying to shake the unease that came with every choice.

My father's men were waiting downstairs in the black sedan they'd used to drive me here. Their presence lingered like a shadow I couldn't escape.

I wasn't just Alessandra. I was Alessandra Navarra. And people like Steven Porter didn't belong in my orbit.

But as I grabbed my key and stepped out to retrieve the last of my things, I felt the pull of something I hadn't let myself feel in a long time: curiosity.

Chapter 3

Coffee and Chemistry

Steven

The café wasn't far from campus, tucked on a quieter side street that felt removed from the nonstop energy of the city. It had mismatched furniture, a faded chalkboard menu, and the kind of coffee that didn't try too hard to impress you. I grabbed a table near the window, more out of instinct than strategy, and watched the street while I waited.

Orientation had been the usual whirlwind: icebreakers, schedules, mildly awkward introductions. There was a buzz in the air, the collective energy of hundreds of people gearing up for a new chapter. But even with all that noise, I kept thinking about Alessandra.

I spotted her the second she walked in. Her movements both calm and deliberate caught my eye. She ordered, waited for her drink, then scanned the room. When her eyes landed on me, she smiled. Not overly warm, but enough to make me sit up straighter.

"Hey," I said as she walked over, keeping it casual.

"Hi," she replied, sliding into the seat across from me. "Hope I didn't keep you waiting."

"You're good. I was early anyway. Needed to scope out the best table, you know?"

She gave a faint smile. "Well, you picked a good one."

There was a pause as we both adjusted, the natural rhythm of two people still figuring each other out. I let it linger a moment before breaking the ice.

"So, orientation. What'd you think?"

She shrugged, brushing a strand of hair behind her ear. "A lot of talking. A lot of walking. Pretty standard."

"Fair," I said. "They throw a ton of information at you and expect you to just absorb it all."

She tilted her head slightly. "I guess it's their way of keeping us too busy to panic."

That made me laugh. "Good point. Personally, I kind of like the chaos. Keeps things interesting."

Her eyes flicked to mine. "Do you always thrive in chaos?"

I grinned. "I like a challenge. Guess that's why I want to be a journalist."

She didn't respond right away, like she was deciding how much to show. When she finally spoke, her tone was thoughtful. "That sounds intense. You don't strike me as someone who'd want to stir things up."

"Really?" I leaned in. "What do I seem like, then?"

She raised an eyebrow. "I'm not sure yet."

I let the moment sit, intrigued. "For the record," I said, "I think the best stories are the ones people don't want you to tell. The ones that make them uncomfortable."

Her expression shifted, just for a second, but enough to make me notice. She glanced toward the window, then back at me. "That sounds risky."

"I'm sure it can be," I said. "But if you're not taking risks, are you really living?"

She traced the edge of her coffee cup, quiet for a beat. Then I saw the moment close behind her eyes.

"What about you?" I asked. "What's your big plan?"

She hesitated. Her posture changed, like answering that meant giving something away. "Honestly? I don't know yet. Still figuring it out."

"Fair enough. Most people don't have it all mapped out, no matter what they say."

She looked at me, a faint smile curving her lips. "What about you? Do you have it all figured out?"

"Not even close," I said. "But I know what I want to chase. That's a start."

She nodded, gaze dropping to the table. A quiet settled between us that wasn't necessarily awkward, but not entirely comfortable either. It felt like she was keeping a wall up, but whether that was deliberate or instinct, I couldn't tell.

"You seem like someone who doesn't wait around," she said.

I raised an eyebrow. "That a compliment or a warning?"

"Depends," she said, her tone light but not playful.

I smiled but didn't press. Clearly, she wasn't someone who gave easy answers.

We shifted to safer topics: classes, books, the usual chatter. But even then, something about her kept me leaning in. She wasn't just guarded; she was intentional, like every word was weighed before she gave it away.

When it was time to leave, I offered to walk her back to campus. She paused just long enough to make me wonder if she'd say no, then nodded.

The walk was quiet. Our steps fell into an easy rhythm,

but I could feel the space she was holding between us. When we reached the dorm, she turned to face me. Her expression was neutral, but not cold.

I wasn't sure what it was about Alessandra that intrigued me. Maybe it was the way she moved through the world like she was holding a map no one else could read. Whatever it was, I didn't mind the wait.

Some stories take time. The good ones always do.

Chapter 4

Between Two Worlds

Alessandra

The walk back to the dorm was quiet, even with Steven right beside me. He was talking about something light and casual, but I only caught fragments of it. My focus kept slipping to the rhythm of our steps and the strange ease I felt in his presence. It wasn't something I let myself feel often.

He had this way about him, this groundedness that didn't quite fit with the chaos of the city or the noise of campus life. It made me want to relax, to drop the carefully measured responses I'd been trained to give. But I couldn't.

When we reached the dorm, I paused outside the door, turning to face him. He stopped too, his hands in his pockets, his posture loose but attentive.

"Well," he said, his easy smile lighting up his face, "thanks for humoring me with the coffee."

"It was nice," I admitted, keeping my tone casual. "A good break from the craziness."

"Maybe we'll make it a habit," he said, his voice light, like he was testing the waters.

I smiled, but I didn't answer. There was a quiet expectation in the air, one I didn't know how to handle. The safest thing to do was end the moment before it became something else.

"See you later, Steven," I said, my hand already on the door.

"Alright," he replied, his tone easy but still holding that edge of curiosity. "See you later, Alessandra."

I slipped inside as he turned around to head for the library. When I made it to my room, I just stood there, staring at the blank walls. The space felt smaller than usual, the air heavier.

I dropped my bag on the bed and sat down, running a hand through my hair. The conversation with Steven replayed in my mind. His relaxed demeanor. The way he seemed sure of himself without being arrogant. It was refreshing. And that was the problem.

He wasn't supposed to feel refreshing.

I shook my head, forcing the thought away. My phone buzzed on the bed beside me, pulling my attention back to reality.

Father: Be at dinner by 6.

The message was as cold and succinct as ever. No pleasantries, no unnecessary words. My father communicated with me the same way he ran his business—precisely and without emotion.

I changed clothes, fixed my hair, and grabbed my room key from my desk and headed out the door. The hallway was mostly empty, the noise from the day fading into the background.

Outside, the familiar black sedan waited at the curb, one of my father's men leaning casually against the driver's side.

He straightened when he saw me, opening the back door without a word. I slid inside, the scent of leather and the faint hum of the engine greeting me like old habits.

The drive to the estate was quiet, the city's energy blurring into the background as we headed north. When the gates came into view, my stomach tightened, the familiar weight of expectation settling on my shoulders.

Inside, the house was just as I'd left it—immaculate, imposing, and utterly devoid of warmth. The staff moved silently through the halls, their eyes downcast, their steps quick.

Dinner was waiting in the smaller dining room, where my father sat at the head of the table. The room was pristine, as always, the table set as if we were expecting company. But it was just the two of us.

"Are you settling in at school?" he asked as I took my seat, his tone as even as his expression.

"Yes," I said, keeping my voice steady. "Everything's fine."

"Good," he said, his gaze sharp. "You know why you're there."

"Yes," I replied, the answer automatic. It was a script I'd known by heart for years: learn, observe, build connections that could one day strengthen the Navarra legacy.

He leaned back in his chair, studying me for a moment. "I heard you're already spending time with your classmates."

My stomach clenched, but I didn't let it show. Of course, he knew without me having said a word. He always knew because I was always being watched.

"I've met a few people," I said carefully. "It's part of the experience, isn't it?"

"Close connections," he said, the word carrying an edge of disdain, "become entanglements. And entanglements are a distraction. A liability. You're not there to make friends, Alessandra. Remember that."

"I know," I said quickly, keeping my tone neutral. "I haven't forgotten."

"Good." He turned his attention back to his plate, the conversation seemingly over.

Dinner continued in silence, the air between us heavy with unspoken expectations. I focused on the delicate pattern of the china, forcing myself to eat even though my appetite had long since disappeared.

Afterward, I excused myself, wandering through the halls until I found myself in the small sitting room at the back of the house. The windows overlooked the gardens, their edges softened by the moonlight. It was one of the few places in the estate that felt remotely peaceful.

I stood there for a long time, my thoughts drifting. Steven's voice lingered in my mind, the memory of his easy smile and his warm, unguarded curiosity cutting through the coldness of my father's words.

But I couldn't let myself get caught up in those moments. They weren't real. They couldn't be.

As I left the estate and headed back to campus, the city lights blurred past the window, their brightness doing little to lift the weight pressing down on me. When we reached the dorm, the guard didn't say a word as he opened the car door. I nodded in acknowledgment, heading inside without looking back.

The hallway was quiet, the buzz of the day long gone.

When I reached my room, I hesitated, glancing down the hall toward Steven's door.

I shook my head, stepping inside and locking the door behind me. There were lines I couldn't cross, no matter how much I might want to.

Steven didn't belong in my world. And I couldn't afford trying to belong in his.

Chapter 5

Getting in too Deep

Steven

The first few weeks of college blurred by in a constant shuffle of classes, late-night study sessions, and navigating the maze of campus life. Somewhere in the middle of it all, Alessandra became a recurring thread, woven into my days in ways I didn't expect.

At first, we ran into each other in passing outside lecture halls, in the library, walking across campus. We'd exchange quick hellos, maybe share a laugh, but nothing more. Slowly, though, those brief moments stretched into longer conversations. Before I realized it, grabbing lunch together had become a habit, something that felt effortless, like we'd known each other longer than a few weeks.

She was different. Alessandra wasn't loud or overbearing like some of the people I met early on. She had this quiet charm, the kind that made you pay attention when she spoke. Her humor was dry, her observations sharp, and there was an intensity to her that I couldn't quite put into words. She didn't open up easily. But when she let a smile linger or shared something that felt personal, it made me want to stay in her orbit just a little longer.

Still, it was hard not to notice the way she held back. Sometimes her gaze would flicker when a conversation got too personal, or she'd pause mid-sentence, like she was choosing her words carefully. She wasn't just private; she was deliberate. And that only made me more curious.

One afternoon, we ended up at Washington Square Park, lounging on the grass with coffees between classes. The late summer sun filtered through the leaves overhead, the faint hum of street performers drifting in from the other side of the park.

"So," I said, leaning back on my elbows, "what's the best book you've read lately?"

Alessandra looked at me, clearly surprised by the question. Her lips curved into a small, thoughtful smile, and I could see her deciding how much to share.

"That's a tough one," she said eventually, tilting her head. "But if I had to pick... probably *The Shadow of the Wind* by Carlos Ruiz Zafón."

"That's a solid choice," I said, nodding. "I read it a couple of years ago. The way he writes about books? It made me want to spend a week wandering through old bookstores in Barcelona."

Her smile widened, more genuine now. "Exactly. It's like he turns books into magical artifacts, something more than just paper and ink."

"Totally," I said, feeling a flicker of excitement at the connection. "It's one of those stories that stays with you long after you've finished it. You don't just read it. You live in it."

Her expression softened. For a moment, the tension she usually carried faded.

"That's how I've always felt about books," she said quietly. "They're more than just stories. They help you see the world differently, find pieces of yourself in places you never thought to look."

"Yeah," I said, watching her closely. "When you're in the middle of a great book, the world just falls away. Nothing else matters."

"Exactly," she said, almost wistfully. "No matter what's happening in your life, you can always lose yourself in a story."

Something in her tone gave me pause, like she was speaking from a deeper place than she meant to. "So why aren't you studying literature?" I asked, keeping my voice gentle. "You clearly love it."

Her smile faltered. She looked away, fingers brushing the grass beside her. "Life doesn't always go the way you want it to."

I waited, but she didn't elaborate. The moment passed. I let it go.

"Okay," I said, "if *The Shadow of the Wind* is the best, what's the worst?"

Her eyes lit up again, and the heaviness from before lifted.

"Oh, that's easy," she said, laughing. "I read this book last year that was supposed to be some deep, profound love story. Instead, it was just... people making terrible decisions for four hundred pages."

I laughed with her. "Sounds like a waste of time."

"It really was," she said, shaking her head. "But I guess you can't appreciate the great ones without slogging through a few bad ones."

"True," I said, smiling. "And at least it gives us something to complain about."

We spent the next hour swapping recommendations, quoting favorite lines, and arguing over the merits of certain authors. It was easy. Effortless in a way I hadn't expected.

But even as we laughed, I couldn't shake the sense that Alessandra was always holding something back. She was here, fully present, but there was a wall. I couldn't see it, but I could feel it.

I don't know what made me stop by her dorm that night. We hadn't made plans, and I wasn't the kind of person who did things like that on impulse. But after a long day of classes, I found myself walking down the hall toward her door, telling myself it was casual. No big deal.

When she opened the door, she looked surprised, but not annoyed.

"Steven," she said, her voice light with just a hint of curiosity. "What's up?"

"Hey," I said, feeling a flicker of awkwardness. "I was just passing by and thought I'd see if you wanted to grab some dinner."

She hesitated, her eyes searching mine. I half-expected her to make an excuse. Instead, she nodded and grabbed her jacket from the back of her chair.

"Sure. Let me get my keys."

We ended up at this little Italian place off-campus, the kind that looks unremarkable from the outside but makes food you dream about later. It wasn't crowded, just a few locals who seemed to know the staff by name.

"This is perfect," Alessandra said as we slid into a booth near the back.

"Figured you might like it," I replied. Truthfully, I'd

only been there once before. But it felt like her kind of place. It was quiet, understated, and comfortable.

The conversation came easily, like it always did with her. We skipped small talk and drifted into the kind of conversation that made hours disappear. She told me about her favorite hidden spots in the city, places she went when she needed to think. A little cafe near Union Square. A quiet bench in Riverside Park that caught the best sunsets.

"What about you?" she asked, resting her chin on her hand as she studied me. "What's your escape?"

I thought for a second, swirling my fork through the pasta on my plate.

"It's not really about the place for me," I said. "It's more about the feeling. Like, when I'm wandering the city with my camera, I get this moment where everything else disappears. It's just me and whatever I'm focused on."

"That's... interesting," she said softly. "Most people would say a favorite hangout or a vacation spot. But you seem to find that feeling anywhere."

"Maybe," I said, shrugging. "I think it's more about noticing things. The stuff most people pass by without really seeing."

She was quiet for a moment, her gaze drifting toward the window.

"I get that," she said eventually. "We're always moving forward. I think most of us forget to look around. Or to notice what's right in front of us."

The conversation shifted after that, back to lighter ground. She asked about my family, and I told her about growing up in the suburbs, the weekend trips into the city, and how I'd always felt like I belonged here.

She shared a little about her childhood, but only the outlines. She hinted at a world I couldn't quite picture.

There was something elusive in the way she spoke, like she was offering just enough to keep me interested without giving too much away.

By the time we left the restaurant, the air between us had taken on a quieter tone that was less casual, more reflective.

"So," I said as we neared campus, "thanks for letting me drag you out tonight. Hope it wasn't too much of a detour."

She glanced over at me, her lips curving into a faint smile. "It was a nice change of pace."

At her dorm, she paused in front of the door and turned to me.

"Thanks for dinner," she said, her voice softer now.

"Anytime," I replied, matching her tone.

She lingered like she might say more, then smiled the briefest of smiles before stepping inside.

I stood there for a few seconds, staring at the closed door. Alessandra had a way of letting you close enough to feel like you were getting somewhere, only to retreat just as quickly. She was a puzzle. One I wasn't sure I'd ever solve.

But the more I tried to convince myself to leave it alone, the more I knew I wouldn't.

Chapter 6

A Study in Patience

Steven

The more time I spent with Alessandra, the more I found myself drawn to her. There was something about the way she carried herself that made it impossible not to want to know more. But I knew better than to rush things. If I pushed too hard or too fast, I'd only end up pushing her away. I felt it whenever conversations got too personal. She'd pull back and start to shut down.

So I played it cool, focusing on what I could do: be her friend, keep showing up, and hope she'd let me in when she was ready.

It wasn't easy. There were moments when I caught myself wanting more, feeling the urge to reach for her hand or say something I couldn't take back. But I held it in, telling myself this was enough. For now.

One Saturday morning, I texted her about spending the day in the city. Nothing fancy, just a low-pressure plan to wander and explore. She surprised me by agreeing almost immediately.

When I suggested starting at The Strand, she lit up.

"I haven't been yet," she said, her voice tinged with excitement.

The moment we stepped inside, I saw it in her face. Her eyes widened as she took in the towering shelves, that quiet awe making her seem younger, lighter.

"Where do you want to start?" I asked, letting her take the lead.

She smiled, open and rare. The kind that always caught me by surprise.

"Let's just wander."

For the next hour, we lost ourselves in the stacks. We picked up random books, shared recommendations, and swapped stories about our favorites. Alessandra was completely in her element, and it was impossible not to feel her energy rubbing off on me.

At one point, we ended up in the fiction section. She picked up a worn copy of *One Hundred Years of Solitude*.

"You have to read this," she said, holding it out to me like it was something sacred.

"It's been on my list forever," I admitted, taking it from her.

Her eyes sparkled. "It's one of those books that changes how you see the world. Trust me."

I added it to my growing stack, grinning. "If it doesn't live up to the hype, I'm holding you personally responsible."

She laughed, soft and melodic, a sound that felt like its own kind of treasure.

After the bookstore, we wandered through the city until we stumbled on a small park tucked between two buildings. It felt like a secret. Quiet. Like it didn't belong in the middle of Manhattan.

We sat on a bench beneath a tree, our bags of books at

our feet. The crisp autumn air carried just enough chill to make it feel cozy, the kind of weather that made you want to stay outside a little longer.

For a while, we just talked about everything and nothing. I let her set the pace. She wasn't the type to be rushed.

Eventually, she went quiet, her gaze distant. I watched her for a moment, debating whether to say anything, but curiosity won out.

"What's on your mind?" I asked.

She hesitated, her fingers toying with the strap of her bag.

"It's just... sometimes I wish things could be different."

"Different how?" I asked, keeping my voice steady.

She turned to me, and for a second, I thought she might actually tell me. But then she looked away, a small sigh slipping out.

"I don't know. I guess I just wish life wasn't so complicated."

I wanted to ask what she meant. I wanted to peel back the layers she kept so tightly guarded. But I knew better.

Instead, I reached out without thinking and touched her arm lightly.

"I'm here," I said.

Her eyes dropped to my hand. For a second, I thought I'd misread everything. Then she smiled, and the tension eased.

"Thank you," she said softly. "I don't think I've ever had a friend like you before."

Friend. The word stung more than I expected. But I nodded, forcing a smile.

"I'm glad I can be that for you."

We sat in silence after that. It wasn't awkward. Just

quiet. I told myself it was enough. That the moment meant something. And maybe it did.

By the time I walked her back to her room, the sun was beginning to set.

"I had a great time today," she said when we reached her door, her voice softer than usual.

"Me too," I said. "We should do it again sometime."

She nodded, hesitating like she wanted to say something else. Then she just smiled. Bittersweet. Fleeting. Familiar.

"Goodnight, Steven."

"Goodnight, Alessandra," I said, watching as she disappeared inside.

I stood there for a moment, staring at the closed door. Being with Alessandra always felt like standing at the edge of something. Close enough to see it clearly, never close enough to step inside.

She was a mystery. One I couldn't stop myself from trying to solve.

As I walked down the hall toward my room, I thought about the way she smiled in the park. The way she let her walls slip just enough to show me the person she usually kept hidden.

It wasn't much.

But it was something.

And for now, that was enough.

Chapter 7

Family Over Feelings

Alessandra

The holiday break crept up on me faster than I'd expected. One minute, I was falling into an easy rhythm with Steven, and the next, I was packing my bags for home. I didn't even have the chance to say goodbye. The abruptness left me unsteady, like I was being pulled from one world into another: a harsher, more controlled one.

The car ride to the estate was quiet. Outside, the city lights blurred into streaks of white and gold, but my thoughts stayed fixed on Steven and the way he made me laugh, the way he looked at me like I was someone worth knowing. I tried to hold onto that feeling, but the closer we got to home, the faster it slipped away, replaced by the weight of my father's expectations.

The estate loomed ahead, its grand stone façade cold and unwelcoming. Inside, nothing had changed. The marble floors gleamed, the chandeliers sparkled, and the air felt just as heavy as ever.

"Alessandra," my father's voice greeted me as I stepped into the hall.

He was standing at the base of the staircase, a glass of whiskey in hand, his posture immaculate as always. There was no warmth in his tone, no smile to soften his sharp features.

"Hello, Father," I said, forcing a smile and crossing the room to greet him.

He leaned in for a brief kiss on my cheek, the gesture practiced and perfunctory. "It's good to have you home."

"Thank you," I replied, though it didn't feel like a homecoming.

"Come," he said, motioning toward the dining room. "Let's have dinner."

The table was set with our finest china, every detail meticulous, as if we were hosting guests. But it was just the two of us.

As we ate, the conversation skimmed over polite topics: my classes, plans for the next semester, the weather. But beneath it all, there was a tension I couldn't ignore. A subtle undercurrent that set my nerves on edge.

After the plates were cleared, my father leaned back in his chair, swirling his whiskey. His gaze settled on me, sharp and unyielding.

"You've been spending time with people at school," he said, his tone casual. But I heard the edge beneath it.

My stomach tightened, but I kept my expression neutral. "I've made some friends, yes."

"Friends." He repeated the word slowly, as if it left a bitter taste in his mouth. "It's important to remember who you are, Alessandra. Not everyone you meet will have your best interests at heart."

"I know," I said, my voice steady.

He took a measured sip of his drink, his eyes still locked on mine. "There's one friend in particular I've heard about," he said. "A boy."

The air thickened. I had to fight to keep my face calm.

"I've spent time with several people from my classes and the dorm," I said carefully, sidestepping the trap I could feel closing around me. "We study together. It's nothing serious."

His lips curved into something that wasn't quite a smile. "Good," he said. "Because at your age, certain... arrangements must be considered. The right connections. The right alliances."

The implication was clear, even if he didn't say it aloud. My future wasn't mine to decide. It never had been.

"Of course," I said quietly. "I understand."

"Do you?" His gaze sharpened. For a moment, I felt like I was under a microscope. "Family comes first, Alessandra. Always."

"Always," I echoed, though the word felt hollow.

Later that night, before I could change clothes or relax in the solitude of my room, a sharp knock broke the silence.

"Miss Alessandra," one of the guards said from the other side. "Your father requests your presence downstairs."

My chest tightened. I quickly neutralized the look of panic I was sure had settled on my face. My father never summoned me this late unless it was important—or unless it was something I wouldn't like.

The guard escorted me to the study, his presence a silent reminder that I was never alone in this house. When we reached the door, he knocked once before stepping aside to let me in.

My father stood by the fireplace, speaking quietly with a man I didn't recognize. The stranger had a sharp, calculating air about him. It was the kind of presence that demanded attention.

"Alessandra," my father said, turning toward me. "Come in."

I stepped forward, keeping my head high despite the unease growing in my chest.

"This is Mr. Luca Vitale," he said, gesturing to the man beside him. "An old friend of the family."

"Mr. Vitale," I said, extending my hand with the practiced grace I'd been taught. "It's a pleasure to meet you."

"The pleasure is mine," he said smoothly. His handshake was firm. His smile faint. "Your father has spoken highly of you."

"Thank you," I replied, though the compliment felt more like a transaction than praise.

"We were just discussing the future," my father said. "It's important to align ourselves with those who share our values."

My chest tightened further. The implication was heavy. This wasn't a polite introduction. This was calculated. A test. A reminder.

"I understand," I said, keeping my voice steady. "Family comes first."

"Good," my father said, clearly satisfied. "Luca is someone you should get to know. He has much to teach you."

Vitale's eyes lingered on me a moment too long. His smile widened.

"I look forward to it."

I managed a polite nod, though my mind was already spinning.

When my father finally dismissed me, I all but fled to my room, closing the door behind me with trembling hands. The façade I'd worn all evening cracked, and I sank onto the edge of the bed, my breath coming in uneven bursts.

His words echoed in my mind, each one driving home the truth: he wasn't just making plans for the family. He was making plans for me.

My phone buzzed on the nightstand. I reached for it, my heart skipping when I saw Steven's name.

Steven: Hope you're having a good break.
Can't wait to see you.

I stared at the screen, a lump forming in my throat. His message felt like a lifeline. A reminder that there was a world outside these walls. But it also felt impossibly far away.

Alessandra: Me, too

I set the phone down and stared out at the snow-covered grounds, the chill of the night sinking deep. I didn't know how much longer I could keep this up, all the pretending, balancing these two lives.

But for now, I had no choice.

Chapter 8

Not Really Fine

Steven

When I saw Alessandra for the first time after the break, I knew something was wrong.

She was walking across the quad, her head down, her steps quick and precise. Her usual poise was there, but she looked worn. Pale. Like the break hadn't given her rest—it had taken something from her.

"Alessandra?" I called, picking up my pace. She glanced over, just briefly, then looked straight ahead again.

"Hey," I said as I fell in beside her, keeping my tone easy. "How was your break?"

"It was fine," she murmured, voice low, flat.

I frowned, watching her carefully. Her eyes were distant, the warmth I'd come to know replaced by something heavy. It felt like she was walking beside me and disappearing at the same time.

"You sure?"

She pressed her lips together, then nodded. "Yeah. I'm fine."

I didn't believe her. But I knew better than to push. Alessandra wasn't someone you cornered. She let you in when she was ready or not at all.

"I missed you," I said quietly.

Her steps faltered, just for a second. She glanced over again, something flickering in her eyes.

"I missed you too," she said, softer this time. Like she hadn't meant to say it out loud.

It was enough.

"I've got something for you," I said. "Back at my dorm. Want to come see?"

She stopped, turning to face me fully for the first time. "What is it?"

"You'll see," I said, smiling. "Just trust me."

She hesitated, weighing something I couldn't see, then gave a small nod. "Okay."

The walk was quiet, but not tense. More like... waiting. Like something had shifted.

When we reached my room, I opened the door and stepped inside, motioning for her to follow. She lingered at the threshold, eyes scanning the space as if checking for exits.

I crossed to my desk and picked up the small, wrapped package I'd left there.

"I saw this and thought of you," I said, keeping my tone casual even though my chest had gone tight.

She stepped closer and took it from my hands, unwrapping it carefully. When she saw what was inside, she froze.

It was the special edition of the book she'd admired at The Strand. I'd gone back for it before the break, wanting her to have something that would remind her of that day. Of the way she'd smiled like nothing was weighing her down.

Her breath caught. For a moment, she just stared.

"Steven," she whispered. "I... I don't know what to say."

"You don't have to."

She looked up, eyes shining.

"Hey," I said gently, brushing away a tear that had slipped down her cheek. "What's going on?"

But the tears didn't stop. They came faster, spilling down her face before she could blink them away. I didn't think. I just stepped forward and pulled her into my arms.

"It's okay," I murmured, holding her close, my hand gently in her hair. "You're okay."

She cried like she'd been holding it in for weeks. No sound. Just quiet, shaking breaths and a body that finally gave in. I held her through it, saying nothing else.

When she pulled back, her face was streaked with tears, her eyes swollen.

"I'm sorry," she whispered. "I didn't mean to—"

"Don't apologize," I said, brushing a strand of hair from her cheek. "You don't have to explain."

She nodded, wiping at her face. But the ache in her expression lingered.

"It's just been a lot," she said quietly.

"I get that. But whatever it is... you don't have to carry it alone."

She looked at me then, really looked at me, like she was about to speak. But the moment passed.

"I should go," she said, stepping back.

I wanted to ask her to stay. But instead, I nodded. "I'll walk you."

We didn't talk much on the way, but the silence wasn't heavy anymore. It felt softer. Like something had cracked open, even if only slightly.

At her door, she turned to me.

"Thank you," she said. "For everything."

"Anytime."

She lingered for a second. Then the door opened and one of her dorm mates stepped out, eyes flicking between us.

"There you are," the girl said to Alessandra. "We've been waiting."

Alessandra offered a tight smile, her posture shifting. I watched her pull herself back together in real time.

"Thanks," she said to me, voice clipped now. Then, more quietly: "Goodnight, Steven."

"Goodnight."

The door closed behind her.

I stood there, staring at the space she'd left behind. I told myself tonight meant something and that we'd made progress. That maybe I'd gotten a little closer.

But the truth was, I still didn't know if she'd ever let me in.

Chapter 9

Pushing and Pulling

Alessandra

I couldn't stop thinking about the way Steven had held me, how steady I'd felt in his arms, how everything else had faded away. For a moment, it had felt like freedom.

And that was dangerous.

It made me forget who I was, where I came from, and what it would cost to let someone like him get too close.

The next day, I avoided him.

I took different routes across campus, ducked into rooms when I saw him coming, kept my head down and my thoughts tighter. It was cowardly. But it was also the only way I knew to protect him—and myself.

Still, it didn't stop him from creeping into my thoughts. He was everywhere. The bench in the quad where we'd sat. The corner of the library where we'd argued over books. The sound of his laugh when he wasn't trying to impress anyone.

The more I tried to push him away, the harder it became.

By the time I made it back to the dorm that evening, I was drained. All I wanted was to disappear into my room and pretend, just for a little while, that nothing had changed.

But near the side entrance, I saw him. Not Steven but one of my father's guards.

He stood against the wall, arms folded, face unreadable.

My stomach dropped.

This wasn't a check-in.

"Miss Navarra," he said as I approached, his voice flat and formal.

"Is something wrong?" I asked, keeping my voice even.

He studied me for a moment before replying. "You've been spending too much time with someone outside the family."

My breath caught.

"Your father is concerned."

"He's just a friend," I said quickly, aiming for lightness. "We study together."

The guard didn't blink. "He asked me to remind you of something. Friends are liabilities. You're expected to keep your distance."

The words landed harder than I expected. My spine stiffened. I nodded. "I understand."

"Good," he said, voice lowering. "Family first."

Then he turned and disappeared into the dark.

I stood there, motionless, the cold pressing in as the silence returned. They were watching me. Waiting for me to make a mistake.

When I finally reached my room, I closed the door and

collapsed onto the bed, the tears coming before I could stop them. Hot. Quiet. Violent.

I'd known this would happen. The second I let Steven in. The second I let myself want more.

But knowing didn't make it easier.

I curled into myself, clutching my knees, as the truth settled like ice in my chest.

I was falling for him.

And the worst part wasn't how much it hurt.

It was knowing it couldn't last.

I kept avoiding Steven. Buried myself in schoolwork. Focused on anything that would keep my mind off him.

But it didn't matter. The pull was still there and it was stronger than ever.

He didn't make it easier.

The way he smiled at me in passing, like I was still someone worth looking at. The way his eyes searched mine even when I refused to meet them. He was gentle, patient, dangerous in all the quiet ways I couldn't protect myself from.

And every moment I gave in, even a little, the guard's words echoed in my mind.

He's a liability.

Not just to me. To him, too.

I was walking a tightrope, one step from slipping. Balancing two lives that couldn't coexist. And I could feel it. Something was going to give.

The question was, when it did...

Would I be strong enough to survive it?

Chapter 10

Frustration

Steven

The distance between us was growing, and no matter what I did, I couldn't seem to close it.

At first, it was little things—plans canceled with vague excuses, shorter conversations, a quietness I wasn't used to from her. But it wasn't long before those little things became impossible to ignore.

I told myself she was just busy, that the semester was picking up, but it felt like a lie even as I thought it. There was something she wasn't telling me, something that had her retreating behind walls I didn't know how to scale.

When my texts started going unanswered, the frustration became too much to ignore.

> Alessandra: I'm sorry, Steven. I'm really busy right now. Can we talk later?

That was the last thing I heard from her before she went silent.

I couldn't leave it like that. I needed to see her, to hear

from her face-to-face that she was okay—or that she wasn't, and maybe there was something I could do to help. So I waited for her after class, watching the door like a hawk as students streamed out.

When she finally appeared, her shoulders were tense, her steps quick like she was trying to disappear into the crowd.

"Alessandra," I called, stepping into her path.

She stopped abruptly, her eyes widening in surprise before she quickly masked it. "Steven," she said, her tone neutral. "I didn't expect to see you."

"I've been trying to reach you," I said, keeping my voice steady even though my frustration was starting to bubble to the surface. "You've been avoiding me."

She hesitated, glancing to the side. "I'm not avoiding you. I've just... been busy."

"That's what you keep saying," I replied, my voice firmer now. "But it feels like there's more to it than that. If something's wrong, you can tell me."

Her sigh was barely audible, but the exhaustion on her face was impossible to miss. "It's not that simple," she murmured. "I'm dealing with some things, and I don't want to drag you into it."

"Don't I get to decide that?" I asked, my frustration flaring for a moment before I softened. "I thought we were friends."

Her head snapped up, her eyes flickering with something close to panic. "We are," she said quickly. "I'm not trying to shut you out, Steven. I just... I can't talk about it right now. Please, just trust me."

The word trust lingered in the air between us, heavy and unsteady. I wanted to trust her, wanted to believe that she'd let me in when she was ready. But standing there, seeing the weight she was carrying, it was hard not to feel like I was already losing her.

"Alessandra," I said softly, "I'm right here. Let me in. Please."

For a moment, I thought I'd broken through. Her eyes softened, her lips parted like she was on the verge of saying something important. But then she looked away, her shoulders slumping.

"I know," she said quietly. "And I'm grateful for that. But right now, I just need some space."

The words hit me harder than I expected. Space. The last thing I wanted to give her was the one thing she was asking for. But the exhaustion in her voice, the way she looked at me—it wasn't something I could argue with.

"Okay," I said finally, my voice barely above a whisper. "If that's what you need."

Relief flashed across her face, though it didn't make me feel any better. "Thank you," she said before turning and walking away.

I stood there for a long moment, watching her disappear into the crowd.

I tried to give her space, like she'd asked. I threw myself into schoolwork, hoping that deadlines and projects would distract me from the ache in my chest. But it didn't work.

Every time I saw her on campus—even from a distance—it felt like something inside me twisted. She didn't look at me the same way anymore. She didn't look at me at all.

I wanted to text her, to check in, to let her know I was still here. But every time I picked up my phone, I stopped myself. She'd asked for space, and I wasn't going to be the reason she built her walls higher.

Still, the waiting was agonizing.

I kept replaying the last time we'd spoken, the way she'd said "trust me" like it was both a promise and a plea.

Whatever she was dealing with, it was tearing her apart. And not knowing what it was? That was tearing me apart.

But all I could do was wait.

Chapter 11

The Bargain

Alessandra

I never meant to hurt him. But every time I got too close, fear sank its claws into me, dragging me back to the cold reality of my life. The more I pushed Steven away, the more I saw the confusion in his eyes, the hurt I was causing. And the more it broke me.

I couldn't stop replaying our last conversation. The way he looked at me when I asked for space, the frustration barely hidden beneath his concern—it lingered in my mind long after I should've let it go. He didn't deserve this. But I couldn't keep dragging him closer to something he didn't understand, something that could ruin him.

That night, I barely slept, tossing and turning as my thoughts spiraled. By morning, I knew what I had to do. If I wanted any chance of being with Steven, I had to talk to my father.

The estate loomed larger than ever as the car pulled into the driveway, the iron gates shutting behind me with a finality that always made me feel trapped. No matter how many times I returned, this place never felt like home. It was a fortress—cold, unyielding, and inescapable.

My father was waiting in his study, the smell of leather and cigars thick in the air. He sat behind his desk, impeccably dressed as always, his expression unreadable.

"Alessandra," he said, gesturing for me to sit. "To what do I owe the visit?"

I took a deep breath, forcing myself to meet his gaze as I lowered into the chair across from him. "I need to talk to you about something important."

He leaned back, studying me like he was trying to anticipate my next move. "Go on."

"There's someone I care about," I said carefully, each word deliberate. "Someone I want to be with while I'm at school."

His eyes narrowed slightly, but he said nothing, waiting for me to continue.

"He doesn't know about the family," I added quickly. "And he won't. I just... I want to have this, even if it's temporary. I need to know if you'll allow it."

The silence that followed was suffocating. My father's gaze bore into me, sharp and calculating, and I could feel my heart pounding as I waited for his response.

"Who is this boy?" he asked finally, his voice calm but edged with authority.

"Steven Porter," I said, steadying my voice. "He's a friend. A good person. He has no connection to this world."

"And you intend to keep it that way?"

"Yes," I said firmly.

He tapped his fingers against the desk, his eyes

narrowing further. "You want a relationship with this boy, but he will never know the truth about you. Do you understand what you're asking of yourself?"

"I do," I said, though the weight of it was already suffocating.

My father leaned forward, his gaze cold and unwavering. "You may have your... experience," he said slowly, as though granting me the barest of concessions. "But it will end when your time at school does. And if there's even a hint that he's learning more than he should, I will handle it. Personally."

The words sent a chill through me, but I nodded. "I understand."

"Good." He sat back, his tone turning final. "Family comes first, Alessandra. Always."

"Yes, Father," I murmured.

"You may go."

I stood, my legs shaky beneath me, and left the study with a hollow sense of victory. I had gotten what I wanted—or at least part of it. But as I walked down the long, echoing hallway, I couldn't shake the dread settling in my chest. This wasn't freedom. It was borrowed time, and I knew it wouldn't last.

The ride back to campus was quiet, the sinking sun casting long shadows across the road. I replayed the conversation over and over, the edges of my father's warning sharp in my mind.

He had given me permission, but it came with conditions—ones that felt like chains around my neck. Steven and

I could be together, but only within the bounds my father had set. Only until it no longer suited the family.

As I walked back to my dorm, the relief I'd hoped to feel never came. Instead, there was a heaviness in my chest, a sadness that refused to let go.

I was going to give Steven what I hoped he wanted—what I knew I wanted—but it came at a cost. I would have to lie to him, keep the truth of my life hidden, and all the while, I'd be counting down the days until I had to let him go.

This wasn't a choice. It was a compromise. One that was already breaking my heart.

Chapter 12

Renewed Hope

Steven

I'd buried myself in assignments, late nights at the library, and endless cups of coffee, anything to distract myself from the ache of Alessandra's absence. But nothing worked. She was always there, in the back of my mind, a quiet presence that refused to be ignored.

I kept telling myself to respect her wishes, to give her the space she'd asked for. But it didn't make the waiting any easier.

When the knock came at my door, I barely registered it at first. I was in the middle of writing a paper, the glow of my laptop screen the only light in the room. It wasn't until the second knock—firmer this time—that I finally stood up with a sigh.

"Coming!" I called, dragging my hand through my hair as I crossed the room.

I opened the door, expecting to see one of the guys from down the hall. Instead, it was her.

"Alessandra."

Her name left my lips in a whisper, the sight of her catching me completely off guard. She looked nervous, her dark eyes darting toward the hallway before settling back on me.

"Hi," she said softly.

For a moment, I couldn't move. It felt like time had slowed, like the world had narrowed to just the two of us. Then her words sank in, and I stepped aside.

"Come in," I said, my voice steadier than I felt.

She walked past me, and I closed the door behind her, the air between us crackling with tension.

I turned to face her, unsure of what to say. She was here, after all the silence, all the space she'd asked for—but why?

"I'm sorry," she said, breaking the silence. Her voice wavered, and she clasped her hands in front of her like she was trying to hold herself together. "I know I've been distant. I didn't mean to... I just needed time."

I studied her, trying to read her expression. She looked tired, vulnerable in a way I hadn't seen before. "Time for what?" I asked gently.

"To figure things out," she said, her voice barely above a whisper. "To figure out how I feel."

Her words hit me like a jolt, hope and caution warring inside me. "And?" I asked, not daring to breathe.

She looked up at me, her eyes dark and uncertain, but there was something else there too—something raw, something real. "I want to start over," she said. "I don't want to keep pushing you away. I want more. If you do, that is."

For a moment, all I could do was stare at her, trying to process what she'd just said. Then, without thinking, I stepped closer.

"Are you sure?" I asked, my voice low.

"Yes," she said, her eyes searching mine. "I'm sure."

Something in me broke then—the restraint I'd been holding onto for weeks, the patience I'd tried so hard to maintain. I reached for her, my hand brushing her cheek as I leaned in.

"Alessandra," I murmured, giving her one last chance to pull away.

But she didn't.

She closed the distance between us, her lips meeting mine in a kiss that was equal parts tender and desperate. It wasn't planned or careful—it was raw, a release of everything we'd both been holding back.

Her hands found their way to my shoulders, clutching at me like she was afraid I might disappear. I pulled her closer, one hand tangled in her hair, the other resting on the small of her back. The world around us faded until there was nothing but her—the taste of her lips, the warmth of her body, the quiet, unspoken promise that this moment was ours.

When we finally broke apart, we were both breathless. Her forehead rested against mine, her eyes still closed as she whispered, "I'm sorry it took me so long."

"You're here now," I said, my voice rough with emotion. "That's all that matters."

Her eyes opened then, and I saw the flicker of doubt that hadn't completely disappeared. She was still holding back, still hiding something. But in that moment, I didn't care.

I kissed her again, softer this time, trying to show her what I couldn't put into words. I wasn't going anywhere.

Alessandra

As Steven's lips met mine, I felt something inside me crack open. The walls I'd spent so long building, the defenses I'd so carefully constructed—they all crumbled under the weight of this moment.

I'd told myself I was here to start fresh, to ask for a second chance. But this kiss, this connection—it wasn't a beginning. It was an unraveling, a surrender to the feelings I'd been trying so hard to bury.

When we finally broke apart, I rested my forehead against his, my breath shaky. "I'm sorry it took me so long," I whispered, the words spilling out before I could stop them.

He pulled back just enough to meet my gaze, his expression soft but intense. "You're here now. That's all that matters."

His words sent a pang of guilt through me, even as they filled me with warmth. He didn't know the whole truth—about me, about my family, about the limits of what we could have. And for now, I couldn't tell him.

But as he kissed me again, his lips gentle and patient, I let myself believe—just for a moment—that this could work. That I could have this one piece of happiness, this one borrowed moment of normalcy, before reality crept back in.

For now, that had to be enough.

Chapter 13

Terms and Conditions

Steven

Dating Alessandra should've been a dream come true. After months of uncertainty, mixed signals, and moments where I wasn't sure if she'd ever let me in, I finally had what I wanted—her. But it didn't feel as simple as I'd imagined.

Our first official date was a quiet, understated affair. Dinner at a tucked-away restaurant off campus, the kind of place where no one would recognize us and we could just be ourselves. She smiled more that night than she had in weeks, and for a little while, I let myself believe that everything was falling into place.

But as the conversation deepened, the easy rhythm between us started to shift. I could feel it—the way her eyes lingered on mine, hesitant, like she was building up to something she wasn't sure how to say.

"Steven," she said, setting her fork down. Her voice was soft, but there was a weight behind it that made my chest tighten.

I leaned forward instinctively. "Yeah?"

She took a breath, and for a second, I thought she might back out. But then she looked up, her dark eyes locking onto mine. "If we're going to make this work, I need you to promise me something."

"Of course," I said, though my voice was careful. "What is it?"

Alessandra's gaze faltered, dropping to the napkin she was fidgeting with. "I need you to promise that you won't ask questions about my family or my past. That you won't dig into things I'm not ready to talk about."

Her words landed like a punch to the gut, stealing the air from my lungs. She was framing it as trust, as a necessary condition for us to work. But I couldn't ignore the unease creeping up my spine.

"Alessandra..." I said slowly, trying to keep my voice steady. "Why is that so important to you?"

She looked up, and for a moment, her walls cracked just enough for me to see the fear behind them. "Because there are things about my life that are... complicated," she said, her voice barely above a whisper. "And I need to know that you trust me enough to let them stay in the past, at least for now."

Complicated. The word echoed in my mind, vague and unhelpful, a black box I wasn't allowed to open. I wanted to argue, to tell her that trust was a two-way street, but the way she looked at me—pleading, vulnerable—stopped me cold.

"Okay," I said finally, though the word felt heavy in my throat. "I promise."

Her shoulders sagged in relief, and she reached across the table to take my hand. Her fingers were warm, trembling slightly, and when she squeezed my hand, it was like she was silently begging me to understand.

"Thank you," she whispered. "That means more to me than you know."

I squeezed her hand back, forcing a small smile. But deep down, doubt was gnawing at me. I'd promised her I wouldn't ask questions, wouldn't push for answers, but I couldn't shake the feeling that I was stepping into something I didn't fully understand.

We finished the night on a lighter note, walking back to campus and laughing about nothing in particular. But even as we tried to recapture the ease of our earlier friendship, the weight of her request hung between us, a shadow I couldn't ignore.

For a while, things felt almost normal. We settled into a rhythm, spending time together like we used to but with the added intimacy of stolen kisses and quiet moments that felt just for us. Late-night coffee runs, aimless walks through the city, hours spent in each other's company—it was everything I'd wanted.

But no matter how much I tried to focus on the present, the promise I'd made loomed over me.

Every time she mentioned something vague about her family in passing or deflected a question about her past, that tension inside me grew. My instincts—the part of me that wanted to know, to understand—kept tugging at the edges of my restraint, daring me to break the promise I'd made. But I couldn't.

Because as much as the secrecy bothered me, the thought of losing her was worse.

Still, the doubt lingered. How could I trust someone who was so determined to keep me at arm's length? How could I give her my heart when she was holding so much of herself back?

It scared me—because I was falling for her. Hard.

The deeper I fell, the more I realized how much I didn't know about the woman I was giving my heart to. And that scared me more than anything. Because love and secrecy? That's not a combination that leads to trust.

One night, as we sat together in the park, the city lights twinkling in the distance, I found myself watching her as she stared out at the skyline. She looked peaceful, but there was something in her expression—a sadness, a weariness—that never quite went away.

"What are you thinking about?" I asked, breaking the silence.

She glanced at me, her lips curving into a soft smile. "Just... everything," she said vaguely.

It was an answer designed to keep me at bay, and I knew it. But instead of pressing, I just nodded, leaning back on the bench.

I'd told myself I could be patient, that I could wait for her to be ready to share. But the waiting was wearing me down. And as much as I wanted to believe in her, to trust that she'd tell me the truth when she was ready, I couldn't ignore the nagging doubt that someday, if she never divulged the truth, those secrets would come between us for the worse.

For now, I kept my promise. I pushed the doubt aside and held on to the moments we shared, hoping that when the time came, Alessandra would trust me enough to let me in.

But a part of me couldn't shake the fear that by the time she was ready, it might already be too late.

Chapter 14

Not too Close

Steven

The semester ended in a haze of finals, late-night study sessions, and packing. It felt strange leaving the dorms behind, knowing I wouldn't be returning to the same routines or the room that had become my home. The promise of summer was a relief—no classes, no deadlines, just a break. But even as I left campus, my mind was already lingering on the one thing that felt anything but settled: Alessandra.

Being home brought some comfort, though. My family's house was just an hour away, close enough to feel connected but far enough to keep some independence. My dad's cancer was manageable for now—not in remission, but stable. Seeing him laugh at one of my mom's jokes or quietly sip his coffee while reading the paper felt like a small victory.

I spent most of my time helping Mom with things around the house. Dad couldn't handle much anymore, and while he tried to laugh it off, the reality of his illness was always there, lingering in the air like a shadow.

It felt good to step in and help—fixing the fence gate, repainting the porch, taking care of the things Dad used to do without a second thought. On his good days, we'd head out to the park or drive to the lake where he used to take me and my brothers fishing. Those days felt like stolen moments of normalcy, like pieces of a life we were all trying to hold onto.

But no matter how much I tried to sink into the comfort of home, Alessandra was always in the back of my mind. We'd been texting and calling, but something about her felt... restrained. It wasn't exactly distance, but it wasn't closeness either. There was still that invisible wall she kept up, one I hadn't yet figured out how to break.

After a few days of unpacking and catching up with my family, I decided to invite her to stay for a week. It felt like the perfect way to bring her into my world, to let her see the parts of me that didn't revolve around school or late-night coffee runs. When I called to ask, she hesitated, and for a moment, I thought she might say no.

"That sounds nice, Steven," she said finally, her voice soft. "But are you sure it's okay with your parents?"

"Of course it is," I said, leaning into a light tone to reassure her. "They've been hearing about you nonstop—they're excited to meet you."

She laughed softly, but I could still hear the hesitation. "I'd love to come, but... I have a favor to ask."

"Anything," I said without thinking, meaning it.

"Could you ask them not to bring up my family? I know it's a lot to ask, and it's not fair to you or them, but... it would make me feel more comfortable."

Her request caught me off guard. I'd learned not to pry

when it came to Alessandra, but that didn't mean I liked having to make this ask of my family. Still, I didn't hesitate. "Of course. I'll talk to them. Don't worry about it."

"Thank you," she said, relief softening her voice. "I'm sorry, Steven. I know it's a big ask."

"Don't apologize," I said firmly. "I understand, and I'll handle it."

After we hung up, I sat with her words for a while, trying to make sense of the request. I knew my parents wouldn't love the idea—openness was a cornerstone of our family—but I also knew they'd respect her wishes for my sake.

That evening, I brought it up with my mom while we were sitting on the porch, watching the last rays of sunlight fade.

"Mom, can I ask you something?"

She glanced over, concern flickering in her eyes. "What is it, honey?"

I rubbed the back of my neck, searching for the right words. "Alessandra's going to come stay for a week. She's really looking forward to meeting you and Dad. But... she asked if we could avoid bringing up her family."

Mom's brow furrowed slightly. "Why would she ask that? Is everything okay?"

"Yeah, everything's fine," I said quickly. "It's just... she says her family situation is complicated, and she's not ready to talk about it. I know it's not a typical request, but it's important to her."

She was quiet for a moment, her gaze steady as she processed what I'd said. "Steven, we'll respect her wishes. You know that. But are you sure everything's alright?"

I nodded, though I honestly had no idea if everything was alright. I could only make assumption based on what

Alessandra had told me—which wasn't much. "I think she just needs time, Mom. That's all."

Mom reached over and squeezed my hand. "We'll follow your lead. If this makes her more comfortable, that's what we'll do. We just want you to be happy."

"Thanks, Mom," I said, relief washing over me.

The day Alessandra arrived, I waited on the porch, scanning the driveway. When a sleek silver Porsche pulled up, I blinked, wondering if I was seeing things. The car was the kind of luxury you only saw in movies or on TV—definitely not what I'd pictured for Alessandra.

The engine purred quietly as it idled, and for a moment, I just stared. Then the driver's side door opened, and she stepped out, looking completely at ease, like she belonged behind the wheel of that car.

"Hey," she said with a small smile, brushing a strand of hair behind her ear.

"Hey," I replied, trying to play it cool. "Nice ride."

She smiled again, but it didn't quite reach her eyes. "Thanks."

I wanted to ask her about the car—how she'd gotten it, why she'd never mentioned it—but I held back, remembering the promise I'd made. Instead, I stepped forward and hugged her, feeling her relax slightly in my arms.

"I'm glad you came," I murmured.

"Me too," she said, her voice soft.

When we pulled apart, her hands lingered lightly on my arms, her eyes meeting mine. For a moment, everything around us seemed to fade—the sounds of the neighborhood, the heat of the afternoon sun. It was just her, standing there in front of me, looking both nervous and completely in control at the same time.

"I missed you," I said quietly, brushing my thumb along her wrist.

Her lips parted slightly, like she wanted to say something, but instead, she just stepped closer. I could feel the tension in the air, the pull that had been building between us for weeks.

Without thinking, I closed the distance between us and kissed her.

It wasn't a rushed kiss. It was soft and slow, and perfect. Her hands slid up to my shoulders, her fingertips brushing against the back of my neck, and for a moment, I forgot everything else.

When we finally pulled away, her cheeks were flushed, her lips curved into a shy smile.

"I missed you too," she whispered, her voice barely audible.

For a second, I just looked at her, wondering how someone could make me feel so grounded and so untethered at the same time. Then, with a deep breath, I nodded toward the house.

"Ready to meet my parents?" I asked, a grin tugging at my lips.

"Ready as I'll ever be," she replied, her smile tentative.

I reached for her hand, giving it a gentle squeeze as we walked toward the door.

As we entered the house, Alessandra hesitated at the door, her steps faltering just slightly. I glanced back at her, offering what I hoped was a reassuring smile. "I'm right here."

She nodded, but the tightness in her expression told me she wasn't.

We stepped into the living room right off the foyer, and gesturing toward my dad, who stood just behind my mom with a friendly but reserved smile, I said, "Mom, Dad, this is Alessandra Romano. Alessandra, these are my parents, Julia and Carl."

My mom greeted us with her usual warmth, stepping forward and pulling Alessandra into a quick hug before she could protest. "It's so nice to finally meet you, Alessandra!"

"It's nice to meet you too, Mrs. Porter," Alessandra said, her voice polite but steady.

"Oh, please, call me Julia," my mom said with a laugh.

"It's wonderful to meet you, Alessandra," my dad said, shaking her hand. His tone was welcoming.

"Likewise," Alessandra replied, her polite smile never faltering.

Mom ushered us into the living room, where she'd set out a tray of snacks and lemonade. Alessandra settled onto the couch beside me, sitting straight, her posture careful but composed.

"So, Alessandra," Mom began as she handed her a glass of lemonade, "Steven's told us so much about you."

Alessandra glanced at me, her smile faint but warm. "All good things, I hope."

"Of course," Mom said brightly, though I noticed the brief flicker of curiosity in her eyes.

Alessandra responded with a soft laugh, and for a moment, the atmosphere felt easy. But as I watched her settle into polite conversation with my parents, I could see the careful way she chose her words, the way her smile didn't quite reach her eyes.

Everything seemed to be going smoothly for now, but I couldn't shake the feeling that Alessandra was holding her breath, carefully navigating my family's warmth and openness like it was enemy territory.

The first few days passed easily enough. Alessandra settled in quickly, joining us for meals and even helping Mom bake cookies one afternoon. She laughed with my parents, entertained my younger cousins when they came over, and even sat on the porch with Dad, listening as he shared old stories about his fishing days.

But as much as she seemed to fit in, I could see the cracks beneath the surface. Whenever the conversation turned to family, her smile tightened, and she deflected questions with practiced ease.

One evening, after dinner, my brothers arrived for the weekend. Nate and Mitch greeted Alessandra like they'd known her for years, but I could tell she was nervous. As we sat around the firepit, roasting marshmallows and swapping stories, she stayed quiet, only chiming in when someone asked her a direct question.

"Alessandra," Mitch said at one point, grinning as he tossed another marshmallow onto his stick, "what about your family? Any embarrassing childhood stories to share?"

The silence that followed was brief but heavy. I saw the tension in Alessandra's posture, the way she glanced at me like she was searching for an escape.

"Oh, I don't know," she said finally, her voice light but distant. "Nothing worth telling, really."

Mitch chuckled, clearly not picking up on her discomfort. "Come on, there's gotta be something."

"She's not gonna top yours, Hay," I interrupted with a laugh, cutting him off before he could push further. "Remember that time you got your head stuck in the railing at the lake house?"

We all laughed and the conversation shifted after that.

But Alessandra remained quiet, her smile fading into something more subdued.

That night, as we sat on the back porch alone watching the stars, I finally broke the silence.

"You've been quiet," I said gently, turning to look at her.

She didn't respond right away, her gaze fixed on the sky. "Your family's amazing, Steven," she said finally, her voice soft. "They're so... open. So warm."

"They love you," I said, reaching for her hand. "They already think you're great."

She smiled faintly, but I could see the sadness in her eyes. "I'm not used to this," she admitted. "Being part of a family like this... it's different."

I wanted to tell her that she didn't have to be different, that she could let her guard down and just be herself. But I knew better.

"I know it's hard for you," I said instead. "I just wish you'd let me be there for you."

Her grip on my hand tightened, but she didn't say anything. Instead, she leaned her head against my shoulder, her silence saying more than words ever could.

Chapter 15

Secrets and Guilt

Alessandra

I had known it would be hard, spending time with Steven's family, but I hadn't realized just how deeply it would affect me. The moment I stepped into their home, I was enveloped by warmth and kindness, the kind of dynamic I had only ever seen from a distance. His mother welcomed me with open arms, his father with a quiet, steady presence that felt comforting in a way I wasn't used to. Even his brothers, who teased Steven relentlessly, made me feel like I belonged—at least on the surface.

But beneath that surface, I felt like an outsider. No matter how much they tried to include me, no matter how much I smiled and laughed along with them, there was always a part of me that remained detached. I couldn't help it. Every time the conversation turned to family—memories of their childhood or plans for the future—I felt the guilt gnawing at me, a constant reminder of the secrets I was keeping from Steven. They didn't even know my real last name. Romano was my grandmother's maiden name, a detail my father had leveraged when he'd pulled strings to keep me hidden in plain sight. It felt like a mask I couldn't take off.

Deflecting their questions was second nature to me, a skill I'd perfected over the years. But here, surrounded by people who wore their hearts on their sleeves, it felt different. It felt wrong.

I wanted to sink into their world, to let myself be carried by the comfort and security they offered. But every time I tried, the weight of my own life pressed down on me, reminding me that I didn't belong. I could pretend, but that's all it was—a pretense. A fragile illusion that could shatter at any moment.

I'd always known this week would be hard, but I hadn't been prepared for the way it would make me feel—like I was teetering on the edge of something I couldn't control. Steven's family was everything mine wasn't: loving, kind, safe. They had welcomed me into their home, their lives, without hesitation, without knowing the truth. And the truth was that I was a liar.

I wasn't the girl they thought I was. I wasn't even Alessandra Romano.

My chest ached with the weight of everything I couldn't say, the secrets I couldn't share. Steven deserved better than this—better than me. But no matter how much I wanted to walk away, I couldn't. Not yet. Not when being with him was the only thing that made me feel like I could breathe.

The house was quiet, the muffled hum of the central air the only sound. The faint scent of lavender drifted up from the freshly laundered sheets, so at odds with the chaos in my mind.

As I stared up at the ceiling, the tears slipping silently

down my cheeks, I made a promise to myself: I would protect Steven from my world, even if it meant breaking my own heart. Because I knew, deep down, that this borrowed time was all we would ever have.

But I wasn't ready to let it go. Not yet.

Chapter 16

Family Matters

Steven

The remainder of the summer passed quickly. Dad had more good days than bad. Mom gushed constantly about Alessandra. Her visit had been perfect on the surface. She'd laughed with my mom, baked cookies in the kitchen, sat on the porch with my dad as he shared stories about his childhood. She fit in so well, it was almost easy to believe she was always meant to be one of us.

Almost.

No matter how much she smiled or how easily she slipped into the rhythm of my family, there was always a distance in her eyes, a guardedness that never fully lowered. And when she went home, it was like that distance widened into a chasm.

We texted and called, but there was a carefulness in the way she spoke, like she was always weighing her words. She never talked about her family, never opened up beyond a certain point. And the more I thought about it, the more it gnawed at me. I thought I'd made peace with not knowing everything, but how long could we keep going like this? What kind of relationship was built on this many secrets?

Toward the end of the summer, I convinced my brothers, Nate and Mitch, to come home for a weekend. They both had their own lives now—Nate with his job at the FBI and Mitch in finance—but when I told them Dad wanted the whole family together, they didn't hesitate.

The weekend was exactly what we needed. We sat around the dinner table telling stories, laughing until our sides hurt. Nate shared a few carefully sanitized anecdotes from his job, while Mitch made us all laugh with his usual sarcastic takes on life in the financial world. Seeing Dad smile like that, really smile, made everything worth it.

After dinner one night, after Dad turned in early, the three of us stayed up in the living room. Nate poured whiskey for himself and Mitch while I stuck to a soda. The three of us sank into the worn-out couch and chairs, letting the conversation flow easily as we caught up on everything from work to old memories.

"So, Steven," Mitch began, swirling the ice in his glass as he grinned at me. "You've been pretty quiet since Alessandra went home. What's the deal with you two? You seemed pretty tight during her visit."

I hesitated, running my thumb along the condensation on my glass as I tried to figure out how to explain it. "We are," I said finally. "It's just... complicated." I was really getting tired of that word.

"Complicated how?" Nate asked, his tone calm but curious.

I sighed, leaning back against the couch. "She's private —really private. Sometimes it feels like there's this whole side of her life that I'm not allowed to be a part of. And it's hard because... I care about her. A lot. But I don't know if I can keep pretending it doesn't bother me."

Mitch's usual smirk softened into something more thoughtful. "Everyone's got their secrets, man. But it didn't seem like there was any distance between you two when she was here."

"That's the thing," I said, frustration creeping into my voice. "When we're together, it feels perfect. But then there's this wall between us. And I have no idea how to break through it."

Nate took a slow sip of his whiskey, his expression steady. "Sometimes people put up walls to protect themselves—or to protect you. It doesn't always mean they don't trust you. It might mean they're not ready to let you carry whatever they're holding."

His words hit harder than I wanted to admit. I thought of Alessandra's face when Mitch had asked her about her family, the way her smile had faltered before she changed the subject.

"Yeah," I said quietly. "But at what point do those walls stop being about protection and start being a problem? Is it ever okay to keep secrets from someone you love?"

Nate set his glass down with a quiet thud. "Deena and I trust each other completely, but there are parts of my job I can't talk about with her. It's not about hiding things—it's about knowing the limits. But you have to ask yourself: Can you live with those limits?"

Mitch shrugged, his tone lighter. "I'm more of a 'no secrets' guy. Tara and I don't have walls between us. Took a lot of growing up to get there, but it works for us. If there's something Alessandra's hiding, you gotta figure out if it's something you can handle—or not."

I leaned forward, resting my elbows on my knees as I

stared at the coffee table. "I don't know," I admitted. "She's it for me. I know that much. But the more I think about it, the more I wonder if there's something she doesn't think I can handle."

We fell into a quiet rhythm after that, each of us lost in our own thoughts. The air in the room felt heavy, the soft hum of the ceiling fan filling the silence.

Nate broke the quiet first, clapping a hand on my shoulder. "Whatever you decide, we've got your back. Always."

"Yeah," Mitch added, his grin returning as he gave me a playful nudge. "And if it all blows up, I'll take you out for a night of wallowing. My treat."

I laughed, the weight in my chest lifting just slightly. "Thanks, guys."

But even as we cleaned up and called it a night, the questions didn't leave me. All I could think about was Alessandra—the way she smiled at my mom, the quiet sadness in her eyes when she thought no one was looking.

I wanted to believe that love could break through anything. But the truth was, I didn't know how long I could keep walking this line—waiting for her to trust me, wondering if the secrets she kept would eventually break us.

All I knew was that I couldn't walk away. Not yet.

Chapter 17

Not Going Anywhere

Steven

The summer faded into fall, and as the leaves began to change, so did the rhythm of life. Back on campus for our sophomore year, I tried to focus on my classes, Alessandra, and the moments we stole away together. We'd found our rhythm again—afternoons tucked into quiet corners of the library, late-night walks through the city, or spontaneous trips to the bookstore when the pressure of school got too heavy.

For a while, it felt easy, like we'd fallen into a world that belonged only to us. But deep down, I knew we were still dancing around the same unanswered questions.

One warm evening, with finals on the horizon, we decided to take a break from studying. The stars were bright overhead as we walked aimlessly through the familiar paths of campus. Alessandra was in a lighthearted mood, laughing at my terrible jokes and teasing me about my exam stress-eating habits. I couldn't help it if cheddar flavored fish-shaped crackers came in gallon sized containers and made the perfect study snack.

As we reached the grove at the edge of campus, I stopped. The canopy of trees overhead gave us a little pocket of privacy, and for once, I didn't feel the usual hum of students passing by.

"Alessandra," I said, turning to face her.

Her laughter softened as she looked up at me, her smile warm and genuine. "What is it?"

I hesitated, nerves coiling in my stomach, but I couldn't hold it in any longer. "I love you."

The words came out steady, but the silence that followed was anything but. For a moment, she just stared at me, her wide eyes catching the moonlight. I could see the surprise there, the flicker of fear that she quickly buried under a soft, hesitant smile.

"Steven..." she started, her voice unsure, but I didn't let her finish.

"You don't have to say it back," I said quickly, trying to ease the tension. "I just needed you to know. I love you, Alessandra. I love the way you laugh and the way you look at me like I'm the only person in the room. An I love the way you seem to carry the weight of everything and still find room to make someone else feel seen. The way you care, even when you don't think anyone notices. You're everything good in my life, and I love all of it."

She bit her lip, her hand instinctively reaching out to mine. "I care about you so much," she said, her voice soft but shaky. "More than you realize. But..."

"But it's complicated," I finished for her, my chest tightening.

She nodded, her grip tightening around my hand. "It is," she whispered, her voice almost breaking.

I took a deep breath and forced a small smile. "I know. And I'm okay with that for now. I'm not going anywhere."

"I'm not sure what love is supposed to feel like," she admitted, her gaze locked with mine. "But when you say it, I want to believe it's this."

I smiled, and for the first time, I saw the wall between us crack—not shatter, but shift. Just a little. And maybe that was all she could give right now, but I could work with that. I could wait for her to find her own way.

"Then believe it," I whispered.

Her gaze locked onto mine, searching, pleading, like she was trying to decide whether I could really handle the truth she carried. Before I could say another word, she closed the space between us, her lips crashing into mine with a force that caught me off guard.

Her kiss was desperate, full of emotion I didn't quite understand. Her hands gripped the front of my shirt, pulling me closer as if I were the only thing holding her together. I kissed her back, pouring everything I had into that moment, hoping it was enough to reach her.

When we finally broke apart, her forehead rested against mine, her breath uneven. "Steven," she murmured, her voice trembling with something I couldn't name.

"It's okay," I whispered, brushing her cheek with my thumb. "Whatever it is, we'll figure it out."

She nodded but didn't speak, the tension in her body telling me that whatever walls stood between us were still firmly in place.

I walked her back to her dorm that night, her hand in mine. She smiled when we said goodnight, but it didn't quite reach her eyes. As I watched her disappear inside, I couldn't shake the feeling that her kiss had been more than a confession. It felt like she was holding on to something that might vanish if she let go.

The semester marched on, and things between us grew quieter, more subdued. Alessandra became harder to read. She smiled when we were together, laughed at my jokes, told me about her classes and her days, but there was a weight in her gaze that hadn't been there before.

Then, one afternoon, I saw her talking to a man I didn't recognize. I'd been on my way to meet her at the library when I spotted them near the older academic buildings.

He was tall, dressed in a dark suit that looked out of place on campus. His posture was rigid, and his expression was stern. Alessandra stood with her back to me, her shoulders tense as she faced him.

From the distance, I couldn't hear their conversation, but it wasn't hard to see that it wasn't friendly. The man handed her an envelope, his jaw tight as he spoke a few more words before walking away. Alessandra stared at the envelope for a moment before tucking it into her bag, her expression troubled.

When I met her in the library a few minutes later, she was all smiles, as if nothing had happened. But the image of that man and the envelope wouldn't leave my mind.

"Everything okay?" I asked carefully as we settled into our usual table.

"Yeah," she replied lightly, pulling out her notes. "Why wouldn't it be?"

I studied her face, but she didn't look up. I wanted to ask her about the man, about the envelope, but I knew how the conversation would go. She'd brush it off, tell me it was nothing, and I'd be left with more questions than answers.

I forced myself to focus on my work, but the doubts gnawed at me. The memory of her kiss, the fear in her eyes, and now this—whoever that man was, he wasn't just "nothing."

Finally, as the library emptied around us, I couldn't keep it in any longer. "Who was the guy you were talking to earlier?"

She froze for just a second before glancing up at me, her expression perfectly neutral. "Just someone from my family," she said casually, her tone light. "It's nothing to worry about."

My stomach tightened. "Are you sure? You seemed upset."

Her smile faltered, but she recovered quickly. "Steven, I'm fine. It's just family stuff. You know how it is."

I didn't, not really. I didn't know what her world was like or why she seemed so afraid of it. But I nodded, forcing myself to let it go—for now.

As we packed up our things and left the library, Alessandra looped her arm through mine, chatting about her plans for the weekend. She was calm, composed, like nothing had happened.

But as I walked her back to her dorm, I couldn't ignore the growing weight in my chest. Alessandra's secrets felt closer than ever, pressing against the fragile surface of our relationship. I'd promised to be patient, to let her open up on her own terms, but I this feeling that I was walking blindfolded into something I didn't understand.

And the worst part was, I wasn't sure how much longer I could wait to find out what was waiting for me in the end.

Chapter 18

Confrontations and Reconciliations

Alessandra

When Steven asked about the man, my heart stopped. I could feel the ground shifting beneath me, the precarious balance I'd been clinging to starting to crumble. The quiet concern in his voice, the way his brow furrowed as he waited for my answer—it was clear he'd seen more than I wanted him to.

But I couldn't let him dig deeper.

The man he'd seen wasn't a stranger; he was one of my father's capos. His warning still echoed in my mind: *You're being watched. Any misstep could cost you—and him.* It was a reminder I didn't need. I lived with that fear every day.

The envelope itself wasn't dangerous; it held concert tickets—a surprise gift for Steven, something I'd planned to remind him how much he meant to me. But the conversation had shaken me, forcing me to confront the fragility of the relationship I was building with Steven. The walls I had erected to protect him weren't just separating him from me—they were suffocating us both.

That evening, as we sat together, I felt the tension radiating from him. I could tell he wasn't going to let it go.

"Alessandra, who was that man?" Steven asked again, his voice soft but insistent.

Panic surged in my chest, and I felt my control slipping. How could I answer the question without getting too close to the truth, to the boundaries I couldn't let him cross? Fear mixed with frustration, spilling out before I could stop it.

"Were you spying on me?" I snapped, my voice sharper than I intended.

Steven blinked, startled, and I saw the hurt flash across his face. "I wasn't spying," he said defensively. "I just... I saw you, and you looked upset."

Guilt clawed at me, but I buried it beneath my fear. "You promised not to pry, Steven," I said, my voice trembling. "You said you wouldn't dig into my past."

"I'm not prying," he insisted, his tone softer now. "I was worried about you. That's all."

His words disarmed me, chipping away at my defenses. I looked at him, at the quiet sincerity in his eyes, and my resolve faltered.

"I'm fine," I said, my voice quieter this time. "It's nothing to worry about."

But he didn't look convinced. His gaze lingered on me, searching.

"I know you're trying to protect me from something," he said quietly. "But it's hard, Alessandra. It's hard not knowing what's going on, not knowing if you're really okay."

The sadness in his voice cut through me, sharp and unforgiving. I wanted to tell him everything—to let him in, to share the burden I'd been carrying alone. But I couldn't. The risks were too high, the stakes too real.

Instead, I reached into my bag and pulled out the envelope, holding it out to him. "Here," I said softly. "This is what he gave me."

Steven took the envelope, his brow furrowing as he opened it. Inside were two tickets to a concert he'd mentioned months ago, something he'd been excited about but never got around to buying.

"For your birthday," I said, my voice barely above a whisper. "I wanted it to be a surprise, but... well, now you know."

I watched as confusion melted into surprise, and then into a warm, genuine smile. The tension in his shoulders eased, and for a moment, the distance between us felt smaller.

"Alessandra, you didn't have to do this," he said, his voice full of gratitude.

"I wanted to," I replied, a small smile tugging at my lips. "I know things have been... tense lately. I just wanted to do something for you."

Without another word, he reached out and pulled me into his arms, holding me close. I let myself sink into the embrace, closing my eyes and wishing, for just a moment, that we could stay like this forever.

"Thank you," he murmured into my hair. "This means a lot."

For a fleeting moment, everything felt right—like we'd turned a corner, like maybe we could find a way through the chaos. But even as I clung to him, I could feel the fear lingering at the edges of my mind, whispering that this peace couldn't last.

"I'm sorry I snapped," I whispered, my voice breaking. "I just... I'm scared, Steven. I'm scared of letting you get too close. I promise it's not because I don't want to. I can't. And I need you to respect that."

He pulled back slightly, just enough to look into my eyes. "I'm not going anywhere," he said firmly, his voice steady and full of love. "We'll figure it out. Together."

I wanted to believe him. God, I wanted to believe him. But the reality of my life was still there, lurking in the shadows. The danger hadn't gone away, and neither had the secrets.

As we pulled apart, I forced myself to smile, even as my heart felt like it was breaking. "You're amazing, Steven," I said softly.

He smiled back, brushing a strand of hair behind my ear. "So are you."

But I wasn't. I was a liar, hiding the truth behind a mask that grew heavier with every passing day.

Later that night, as I lay in bed, the weight of what had happened pressed down on me. Steven's words, his unwavering belief in us—it should have comforted me. Instead, it left me feeling hollow.

Because I knew I couldn't keep this up. The longer I stayed with Steven, the closer I came to putting him in danger. And as much as I loved him—as much as I needed him—I couldn't shake the certainty that the only way to protect him was to let him go.

But not yet. Not tonight.

For now, I would hold onto this fragile illusion of normalcy, knowing it wouldn't last. Knowing it couldn't.

And as I closed my eyes, the tears slipping silently down my cheeks, I made a silent promise to myself: when the time came to say goodbye, I would make sure Steven never looked back.

Chapter 19

The Move

Steven

Junior year started with a flurry of activity. Between classes, work, and settling into our new apartment, it felt like we were constantly on the go. But even with the chaos, there was an underlying excitement—a sense that this was the start of something new, something that could take us to the next level.

Moving in with Alessandra was something I'd been looking forward to for months. The moment we signed the lease on our cozy one-bedroom apartment just off campus, it felt like everything was falling into place. I could barely contain my excitement as I imagined mornings waking up next to her, late nights talking on the couch, and all the little moments we'd share.

The move itself was exhausting but rewarding. We spent hours unpacking, rearranging furniture, and debating where everything should go. By the time we finished, the sun had set, leaving us surrounded by boxes and half-finished ideas for decor. We collapsed onto the couch, breathless and covered in dust, but it felt like an accomplishment—a shared victory that marked the beginning of something bigger.

Alessandra leaned against me, her head resting on my shoulder, her hair brushing my cheek. I wrapped an arm around her and pulled her closer, feeling a wave of contentment settle over me.

"Can you believe we're actually doing this?" I murmured, my voice soft but tinged with disbelief.

She tilted her head up to look at me, her eyes shining. "It feels... surreal," she admitted. "Like I'm still waiting to wake up."

"Well, if this is a dream, I don't ever want to wake up," I replied, pressing a kiss to her forehead.

She smiled at that, the kind of smile that made everything else fade away. For a while, we just sat there, letting the quiet moments stretch between us, the chaos of unpacking forgotten.

"I love you," I breathed out, those three little words slipping from my lips like a prayer. My heart hammered in my chest as I looked into her eyes, searching for any hint of doubt or uncertainty. But all I saw was a reflection of my own desire, burning bright and fierce.

She sighed at the sound of my confession. For a moment, time seemed to stand still as we stared at each other, locked in a standoff of passion and longing. And then, without warning, she reached up to touch my face, her fingers tracing a path along my jawline and sending shivers down my spine.

"I love you, too," she whispered, her voice trembling with emotion.

Those words hit me like a freight train. If I'd been

standing, my knees would've gone weak. I gazed into her eyes, stunned by the love and certainty shining back at me.

I'd told her I needed to hear those words before I could give her all of me, and now she had. The dam inside me broke.

"Again," I whispered, my voice rough with emotion. "Say it again."

"I love you," she said, stronger this time, pulling me to my feet. Her body pressed close to mine, and suddenly nothing else mattered.

Her lips found mine, and the kiss carried all the fire of our longing—but beneath it was something far greater. Trust. Belonging. Love.

We lost ourselves in each other, laughter and whispered promises marking the path ahead. The rest of the world had disappeared.

That night was ours alone, the beginning of something sacred and unshakable.

She turned to me with a soft smile. "I can't believe this is real."

"I love you," I whispered again, brushing a kiss across her lips.

"I love you too," she replied, her voice warm with certainty.

I believed her. And I knew, without a doubt, that my life had changed forever.

Chapter 20

Trapped by Love

Alessandra

Living with Steven was everything I had imagined and more. Waking up next to him every morning, sharing meals, talking about our days—it was like a dream come true. The apartment had quickly become our sanctuary, a place where the world outside faded away and it was just the two of us.

But even in our little bubble of happiness, I couldn't shake the feeling that time was running out. Every time I looked at him, I was reminded of the promise I had made to my father—the deal that hung over me like a shadow, darkening every moment we shared.

At first, I tried to push those thoughts aside, to focus on the here and now. I told myself that I would worry about the future when it arrived, that I would let myself enjoy this time with Steven for as long as I could. But as the weeks turned into months, the weight of that unspoken deadline grew heavier, pressing down on me until it was all I could think about.

I could feel it in the quiet moments, when Steven would catch me staring off into space and ask if I was okay. I could feel it in the way my chest tightened every time he told me he loved me, the words both a balm and a knife to my heart. I wanted so badly to believe that we could make this work, that somehow we could defy the odds and stay together, but I knew better. The life I had been born into was not one that allowed for happy endings.

The breaking point came one afternoon when I received a message from my father, summoning me to the family estate. The tone was formal, as always, but there was an underlying tension that set my nerves on edge. I knew better than to delay, so I made the drive out that evening, my mind racing with possibilities, none of them good.

When I arrived, the estate was as imposing as ever, the grand facade a stark contrast to the turmoil churning inside me. The guards nodded as I passed, their faces impassive, but I could feel their eyes on me, watching, always watching.

When I entered his study, the room was softly lit by a single lamp, where my father was waiting. He didn't rise when I entered, simply gesturing for me to sit. I obeyed, my heart pounding in my chest as I waited for him to speak.

"You've been quiet lately," he began, his voice calm, measured. "I was beginning to wonder if you'd forgotten your obligations."

I swallowed hard, trying to keep my voice steady. "Of course not, Father."

He nodded, as if satisfied with my response, but I knew better than to let my guard down. "You're still seeing that boy," he said, not a question, but a statement. "The one from school."

"His name is Steven," I said, trying to keep the defensiveness out of my voice.

My father's eyes narrowed, and I could see the calculation behind them. "Steven," he repeated, as if tasting the name. "Tell me, Alessandra, are you taking precautions?"

The question hit me like a slap to the face, my cheeks burning with a mix of embarrassment and anger. "That's none of your business," I snapped before I could stop myself.

His expression hardened, his eyes cold. "Everything about you is my business, Alessandra. You would do well to remember that."

I looked away, biting back the retort that rose to my lips. It wasn't worth it, not when I knew how this conversation would end.

"Are you?" he asked again, his tone sharp.

"Yes," I replied, the word bitter on my tongue. "I'm being careful."

"Good," he said, his tone softening slightly. "You're a smart girl, Alessandra. You understand the importance of maintaining control over your life, over your decisions. That's what separates us from the rest of the world—our ability to make the hard choices, to do what must be done."

I nodded, though the words felt hollow. Control. It was a lie, one I had been told my entire life. I had never had control over my life, not really. Every choice, every decision, had been made for me, dictated by the needs of the family, by the rules that governed our world.

"I haven't forgotten what we agreed," I said quietly, forcing myself to meet his gaze. "When graduation comes, I'll end it."

"See that you do," he replied, his tone leaving no room for argument. "And remember, Alessandra, you have a duty to this family. You're a Navarra—don't let yourself forget that."

I left the estate that night feeling more trapped than ever. The drive back to the apartment was a blur, the dark road stretching out before me as my thoughts spiraled. How had it come to this? How had I allowed myself to believe, even for a moment, that I could escape the life I had been born into?

When I arrived home, Steven was waiting for me, concern etched on his face as he pulled me into his arms. "Is everything okay?" he asked, his voice full of the love and warmth that had become my anchor in this storm.

I nodded, forcing a smile as I buried my face in his chest. "It's fine," I lied, the words sticking in my throat. "Just family stuff."

He didn't push, just held me close, his hand gently stroking my hair as if he could soothe away the turmoil inside me. But even as I leaned into his embrace, I felt the walls closing in, the reality of my situation pressing down on me from all sides.

How long could I keep this up? How long could I pretend that we had a future, that I wasn't lying to him every single day? The guilt was becoming unbearable, a constant weight on my chest that made it hard to breathe, hard to think.

I knew what I had to do. I had to end it, to walk away before it was too late—before I hurt him more than I already had. But every time I tried to imagine my life without him, the thought was too painful to bear.

"I love you," he whispered, his breath warm against my skin. "You know that, right?"

"I know," I replied, my voice trembling. "I love you too."

And I did—I loved him more than I had ever thought

possible. But that love was a trap, one that would only lead to more pain, more heartbreak. I was living a lie, and it was only a matter of time before it all came crashing down.

As I lay in bed that night, curled up beside Steven, I stared at the ceiling, my mind racing with possibilities. Could I really walk away? Could I leave him before graduation, before the inevitable end? Or was I too far gone, too deeply in love to save either of us?

The answer, I knew, was one that would haunt me for the rest of my life—no matter what I chose.

Chapter 21

The Ring and the Rift

Steven

Senior year was supposed to be the culmination of everything Alessandra and I had built together—a time to look toward the future, to make plans, and to finally take the next step. But instead of the clarity I had hoped for, all I felt was a growing sense of unease.

Over the summer, my dad had given me a ring that had belonged to my grandmother. It was a simple, elegant piece —timeless, just like her. One Saturday I'd gone home to help my dad get some yard work done. That evening my dad handed me a small velvet box, his eyes misty with emotion.

"This ring was your grandmother's," he said softly. "She had one set aside for each of my boys before she died. This is the one meant for you to give to the person who fills your soul with love and joy."

I had taken the box with reverence, the weight of the ring in my hand feeling like both a blessing and a responsibility. At the time, I was sure I'd use it before graduation, certain that by then, I'd be ready to ask Alessandra to marry me. But as the months passed and graduation loomed closer, doubt began to creep in.

It wasn't that I loved her any less. If anything, my love for her had only grown deeper, stronger, as we navigated the ups and downs of our senior year. But the questions—the ones I had promised not to ask—were becoming impossible to ignore. There were still so many things I didn't know about her, so many secrets she kept locked away, and it was starting to eat at me.

The turning point came the night I had planned to propose. We'd been out for a quiet dinner, a place we'd discovered early in our relationship that had become something of a tradition. The ring had been in my dresser for months, and I'd taken it out that afternoon, my heart pounding as I slipped it into my pocket. This was it—I was going to ask her to marry me.

But from the moment we sat down at the restaurant, something felt off.

Alessandra had been unusually quiet throughout the evening, her mind clearly elsewhere. I knew that she'd seen her father earlier that day, and the tension she carried with her had been palpable. It wasn't the first time she'd withdrawn after one of their meetings, but this time, the silence between us felt different—heavier, more foreboding.

When we got back to the apartment, Alessandra went to bed early, leaving me alone in the living room, staring at my laptop. The ring was in its usual place, tucked away in the back of my dresser drawer, but the weight of it pressed heavily on my mind. What was I waiting for? What was holding me back?

The answer was painfully clear: the secrets. The things she wouldn't tell me, the parts of her life that remained a mystery, even after all this time. I had tried to respect her boundaries, to keep my promise, but the closer we got to graduation, the more I felt like I was standing on the edge of a cliff, unsure whether to take the leap or pull back.

That night, the temptation became too strong to resist. Before I even knew what I was doing, I found myself opening my laptop, my fingers hovering over the keys. I could look her up—just a quick search, a peek into the life she had kept hidden from me. It wouldn't take much. I had the skills, a few resources. I could find out everything I wanted to know in a matter of minutes.

But as I stared at the blank search bar, my heart pounded in my chest. This was exactly what she had asked me not to do. She had trusted me to respect her privacy, to believe in her without needing to know every detail of her past. And here I was, about to betray that trust because I couldn't handle the uncertainty.

My hand hovered over the keyboard, the temptation almost overwhelming. But then I thought about the ring—the one still in my pocket, the one I had been planning to give her tonight. What would she think if she knew I was about to break my promise? How could I ask her to marry me if I couldn't even trust her enough to keep my word?

With a deep breath, I pushed the laptop away, my hand slipping into my pocket to touch the soft velvet of the box. I couldn't do it. I couldn't break my promise, not when I was so close to asking her to spend the rest of her life with me. But the decision brought little relief. The questions were still there, gnawing at the edges of my mind, and I knew they weren't going to go away on their own.

The next morning, Alessandra noticed the change in me. We were getting ready for class when she looked at me, her brow furrowed in concern. "Steven, is everything okay?"

she asked, her voice soft, but laced with that familiar caution.

I hesitated, the words stuck in my throat. I wanted to tell her, to explain how close I had come to breaking my promise, how much it was tearing me apart not to know the truth. But I couldn't. Not without risking everything.

"Yeah, I'm fine," I said, forcing a smile. "Just didn't sleep well."

She didn't look convinced, but she didn't push, either. "If something's bothering you, you can tell me," she said gently, reaching out to touch my arm. "You know that, right?"

"Of course," I replied, but the words felt hollow. I didn't know how to tell her what I was feeling, didn't know how to explain the turmoil inside me without making it sound like I didn't trust her. And that wasn't it—I trusted her more than anyone else in the world. But the secrets... they were eating away at me, bit by bit.

We left for class, but the tension between us lingered. I could feel it in the way she looked at me, in the careful distance she kept. Something was changing between us, and neither of us knew how to stop it.

That evening, when we were back home, she confronted me. We were sitting on the couch, the TV playing in the background, but neither of us was paying attention. Alessandra turned to me, her eyes searching mine.

"Steven," she began, her voice hesitant. "I feel like there's something you're not telling me. Have I done something to upset you?"

Her question hit me like a punch to the gut. She hadn't done anything wrong—if anything, it was my own doubts and fears that were to blame. But how could I explain that to her?

"It's not you," I said quickly, trying to reassure her. "I've just been... dealing with some things."

"What things?" she asked, her tone sharpening.

I swallowed hard, the words lodged in my throat. "It's nothing, really," I tried again, but she wasn't having it.

"Steven, don't lie to me," she said, her voice cracking with emotion. "I know something's wrong. Please, just tell me."

I could see the fear in her eyes, the worry that had been building up, and I hated myself for being the cause of it. But I couldn't tell her—not without risking everything we had.

"It's just... I've been thinking a lot about the future," I said, choosing my words carefully. "About us, and what's going to happen after graduation."

She nodded, but I could see the tension in her posture, the way her hands clenched into fists. "And?"

"And I'm scared," I admitted, the truth slipping out before I could stop it. "I'm scared that I don't know enough, that there's too much I don't understand about your life. I want to be with you, Alessandra, more than anything. But I feel like there are all these walls still between us, and I don't know how to break them down."

Her eyes filled with tears, and I could see the hurt in them. "I thought you trusted me," she whispered, her voice trembling.

"I do," I said quickly, reaching out to take her hand. "I trust you more than anyone. But it's hard, Alessandra. It's hard not knowing, not understanding what you're going through. There are days you go see your father, a man I've never met, and when you get home you look defeated and sad. You stare off into space in silence and I wonder if wherever you go in your mind if I'm even there."

She pulled her hand away, wiping at her eyes. "I told you from the beginning that there were things I couldn't share," she said, her voice tight with emotion. "I thought you understood that."

"I did," I insisted, but the words felt weak. "I do. But it doesn't make it any easier."

The silence between us was thick, heavy with the weight of everything unsaid. I could feel her slipping away from me, and it terrified me.

"I love you," I said desperately, the words tumbling out in a rush. "I love you, and I don't want to lose you."

She looked at me, her eyes searching mine, and for a moment, I thought I saw something break in her. But then she shook her head, standing up from the couch.

"I need some air," she said quietly, and before I could respond, she was gone, the door closing softly behind her.

I sat there for a long time, staring at the empty space where she had been, my heart aching with the knowledge that I had just brought us to the brink of collapse. The ring back in the drawer felt like a distant memory, a dream that was slipping away with each passing day.

How had it come to this? How had we gone from planning a future together to standing on the edge of something neither of us knew how to fix?

I didn't have the answers, but I knew one thing for sure: I needed her and I'd do whatever I needed to make her see she could trust me.

Chapter 22

A Desperate Reality

Alessandra

Senior year was supposed to be the time when everything fell into place. The final stretch before graduation, the culmination of everything Steven and I had built together. But instead of clarity, all I felt was a suffocating sense of dread.

I had known from the beginning that our time was limited, that once graduation came, I would have to end things with Steven. It was part of the deal I had made with my father—my college experience, my chance to taste a life outside the family's grip, would end the moment I walked across that stage to receive my diploma. But knowing it and accepting it were two entirely different things.

The closer we got to graduation, the harder it became to accept. I couldn't stand the thought of losing Steven, of walking away from the only happiness I had ever known. So, instead of distancing myself, I did the opposite. I threw myself into our relationship, determined to make the most of every moment we had left.

I became the perfect girlfriend. I cooked his favorite meals, and showered him with affection. Every time he looked at me, his eyes filled with love and gratitude, it made my heart ache with a bittersweet mix of joy and sorrow. I wanted to make him happy—I needed to. But the more I tried, the more it felt like I was desperately trying to hold onto something that was already slipping through my fingers.

One evening, I surprised him with a candlelit dinner at our apartment. The table was set with his favorite meal, the lights dimmed to create a warm, intimate atmosphere. Steven walked in, his eyes widening in surprise as he took in the scene.

"What's all this?" he asked, a smile tugging at the corners of his mouth.

"Just thought we could use a special night," I replied, my voice light as I crossed the room to kiss him.

He kissed me back, his arms wrapping around me as he pulled me close. "You're amazing, you know that?"

I smiled, but it felt fragile, like it could shatter at any moment. "I just want to make you happy," I whispered, my heart aching with the weight of the words.

"You do," he said, his voice full of sincerity. "You make me happier than I ever thought possible."

We sat down to eat, the conversation flowing easily between us. But even as we talked and laughed, a part of me was consumed by the knowledge that this couldn't last. I was living a lie, trying to pretend that everything was normal, that we had a future together. But the truth was always there, lurking at the edges of my mind, ready to pounce the moment I let my guard down.

After dinner, we moved to the couch, our bodies curled together as we watched a movie. But my mind wasn't on the screen. I kept thinking about the deal I had made with my father, the promise I had given him to end things with Steven after graduation. The thought of it made me sick to my stomach, and I found myself wondering—what if I could change his mind?

My father had always been strict, unyielding in his expectations. But I had seen moments of softness in him, glimpses of the man he might have been if our lives hadn't been dictated by the family business. What if I could appeal to that side of him? What if I could convince him that Steven wasn't a threat, that we could be together without it affecting the family?

It was a dangerous line of thinking, I knew that. But the more I thought about it, the more I clung to the hope that maybe—just maybe—I could find a way to keep Steven in my life.

Steven must have sensed the tension. He turned his head and asked, "What are you thinking about so hard over there?"

Faking a smile, I said, "You."

His eyes darkened and a smirk played at his lips. "Yeah? What exactly are you thinking?"

"I'd rather show you," I whispered, pushing the heavy thoughts from my mind.

I kissed him, needing the distraction, needing him. His arms wrapped around me, his kisses growing more urgent, and the world narrowed to just the two of us. Every touch, every laugh, every whispered promise carried a desperation I couldn't quite hide. Any night could be our last, and I wanted to hold onto each one as if it might slip away.

We moved together with a kind of reckless tenderness, clinging tightly as if we could make time stop. For that moment, nothing else mattered—no looming threats, no future we couldn't control—just the certainty of his love and the warmth of his embrace.

The night was ours alone, etched into memory with a depth words could never capture.

When we finally stilled, laughter and quiet breaths filling the room, Steven brushed a strand of hair behind my ear and whispered, "You really are amazing."

I smiled up at him, my heart full and aching at the same time. "You can think about me like that anytime," he teased softly.

He pulled me closer, his lips brushing mine again. And for that fragile, fleeting stretch of time, there was nothing else in the world but us.

As we cuddled together on the couch, Steven whispered softly in my ear, "I love you."

My heart clenched at those words. I loved him too—more than anything—and yet here we were on borrowed time.

"I love you too," I whispered back.

The next morning, I made the drive out to the estate, my mind racing with what I was going to say. I hadn't told Steven where I was going, just that I had some errands to run. He had looked at me with that same mix of love and concern, and it had taken everything in me to hold back the tears.

When I arrived, the estate was as imposing as ever, the grand facade a stark reminder of the life I was bound to. The guards nodded as I passed, their faces impassive, but I could feel their eyes on me, always watching.

My father was in his study, as usual. He didn't rise

when I entered, simply gesturing for me to sit. I obeyed, my heart pounding in my chest as I tried to find the words.

"What brings you here, Alessandra?" he asked, his voice calm, measured.

"I wanted to talk to you about Steven," I began, my voice trembling slightly.

His expression didn't change, but I could see the flicker of something in his eyes—curiosity, maybe. Or was it suspicion? "What about him?"

"I know what we agreed," I said, choosing my words carefully. "But I was hoping... maybe we could reconsider. Steven isn't a threat, Father. He doesn't know anything about the family, and he never has to. He's a good man, a kind man, and I love him."

My father's eyes narrowed, and I could see the cold calculation behind them. "You know what's at stake, Alessandra. Our world is not one that allows for weaknesses, and love is a weakness. I made that clear from the beginning."

"I know," I said quickly, my heart sinking. "But—"

"There are no buts," he interrupted, his voice sharp. "You made a deal, and you will honor it. Or have you forgotten what happens to those who betray the family?"

The threat hung in the air between us, heavy and unmistakable. I knew better than to push further. My father's word was law, and once he had made up his mind, there was no changing it.

"I understand," I said quietly, my voice hollow.

"Good," he replied, his tone softening slightly. "You're a smart girl, Alessandra. You know what's best for the family."

I left the estate that day with my hopes crushed, my heart heavy with the knowledge that there was no escape. I had tried, but the door had been slammed shut in my face. Steven and I were living on borrowed time, and no amount of love or affection could change that.

When I got back to the apartment, Steven was waiting for me, concern etched on his face. "Are you okay?" he asked, pulling me into his arms.

I nodded, forcing a smile. "I'm fine," I lied, the words bitter on my tongue, even though I should be used to them.

He didn't push, just held me close, his hand gently stroking my hair as if he could soothe away the turmoil inside me. But even as I leaned into his embrace, I felt the walls closing in, the reality of my situation pressing down on me from all sides.

The weeks that followed felt like a dream I was desperate to cling to, even as it began to unravel at the seams. I threw myself into our relationship, determined to savor every moment we had left. Elaborate dates, surprise breakfasts in bed, nights spent laughing until we were breathless—I poured everything I had into creating memories we could both hold on to.

Steven noticed, of course. He was too perceptive not to. His questions came like gentle waves, but each time, I brushed them aside with a smile or a joke, assuring him that I was fine, that we were fine. I didn't want to ruin what little time we had left by speaking the words that would shatter it all.

But the weight of my secrets was suffocating, an ever-present ache that stole my breath and clouded my thoughts. Graduation was looming, and with it, the end of everything I had come to cherish. Every time Steven talked about our future—about plans for the summer or ideas for grad school—I felt the crushing weight of what I couldn't say.

Still, I couldn't bring myself to walk away. How could I,

when he was the only light in a world that felt so dark? How could I let go of the one thing that made me feel human when everything else seemed determined to pull me under?

One night, as I lay awake beside him, his soft breaths filling the quiet room, I stared at the ceiling, my thoughts racing. I'd tried to carve out a different path, to fight for something more. But the truth was staring me in the face with chilling clarity: there was no way out.

The life I had been born into wasn't something I could escape. My father's words echoed in my mind, a grim reminder of the line I couldn't cross.

Steven stirred beside me, his arm draping over my waist as he mumbled something in his sleep. I turned to look at him, the soft lines of his face illuminated by the moonlight streaming through the window. He looked so peaceful, so unburdened, and the sight of him like that—so vulnerable, so open—nearly broke me.

I wanted to tell him everything. I wanted to lay it all out, to let him see the tangled mess of my life and trust that he would still love me anyway. But I couldn't. Because loving me meant risking everything—his safety, his future, his life. And I couldn't live with myself if I was the reason he got hurt.

As the days stretched on, the weight of the inevitable pressed harder, the countdown ticking louder with each passing moment. I didn't know how much longer I could keep up the facade, how much longer I could pretend that everything was okay.

But one thing was clear: when the time came, it would break us both.

Chapter 23

Almost Over

Steven

Graduation day had finally arrived—a day I'd been dreaming about for months, not just because it marked the end of our college years, but because it was the beginning of something so much bigger. Tonight, if everything went as planned, I was going to ask Alessandra to marry me.

The morning was a whirlwind of celebration. My family had driven down to watch the ceremony, their pride radiating in every hug, every cheer as I walked across the stage to get my diploma. Mom cried, of course, dabbing her eyes with a tissue, while Dad looked like he might burst from smiling so much. Even my brothers, usually quick to tease me, seemed genuinely proud.

As much as I loved sharing this moment with them, my thoughts kept drifting to Alessandra. She had been right there with me all morning, her smile radiant, her eyes brimming with love and pride. We'd made it through college together, and now, standing at the edge of the future, I knew what I wanted next.

I'd thought about proposing so many times before, but something always held me back—doubt, uncertainty, or the weight of the unknowns between us. But today, none of that mattered. Today, I was certain. I couldn't imagine my life without her, and I didn't want to.

After the ceremony, we spent the afternoon with my family, eating, laughing, and sharing stories about the last four years. Alessandra fit in seamlessly, her laughter blending with theirs, her presence lighting up the room. I could so easily picture her as part of my family—sitting at our dinner table during holidays, her hand in mine as we navigated life together.

But as the day wore on, I started to notice a shift. There was something in her eyes—something distant, as if she were somewhere else entirely. When I asked if she was okay, she just smiled and squeezed my hand. "I'm fine," she said, her voice warm but a little too light.

"I've got to see my family this afternoon," she told me as we started to say our goodbyes to my parents. "I'll meet you at the restaurant."

"I can't wait," I said, forcing a grin even as a knot of unease formed in my chest.

She kissed me softly, her lips lingering on mine. "I love you," she whispered, her eyes searching mine.

"I love you, too," I replied, brushing a strand of hair from her face. But as I watched her walk away, that knot in my chest tightened.

Tonight was going to be perfect. I had made sure of it.

After my family said their goodbyes, I headed back to the apartment where I spent the afternoon preparing. I laid out my suit, checked the ring one last time, and rehearsed what I would say. I pictured her face when I got down on one knee—the way her eyes would light up, the way she'd laugh through her tears before saying yes.

I tried not to think about the flicker of doubt I'd seen in her eyes or the tension in her voice when she said goodbye. Whatever was on her mind, I would ease it tonight. I would prove to her that we were meant to be together.

By the time I arrived at the restaurant, the sun was beginning to set, painting the sky in soft hues of orange and pink. The private room I'd reserved was perfect—intimate, with candles flickering softly on the table and a view of the city lights twinkling through the window.

I checked my watch, my heart thudding in my chest. She'd be here any moment. I could hardly sit still, the weight of the ring in my pocket a constant reminder of the life I was about to ask her to share with me.

I let my mind wander back over the years we'd spent together. I thought of late-night study sessions in the library, stolen kisses between classes, lazy Sunday mornings tangled up on the couch. We'd been through so much, and every moment had only solidified what I already knew—I wanted her in my life forever.

I glanced at my watch again, the minutes stretching longer than they should have. She was running late, but I told myself not to worry. She would walk through that door any second now, her smile lighting up the room as it always did.

And when she did, I would ask her to take this leap with me—to trust me, to love me, to build a future together.

I checked my watch again. Five minutes late. Then ten.

I called but there was no answer.

The knot in my chest turned into an ache. Something

felt wrong, but I pushed the thought aside. She wouldn't let me down. She wouldn't miss this.

I adjusted my tie, fidgeted with the napkin on the table, glanced at my watch once more.

Fifteen minutes.

I called and texted, both went unanswered.

The anticipation that had been bubbling all day began to curdle into something cold and uneasy.

I stared at the door, willing it to open, willing her to walk through it, her smile chasing away every doubt that had begun to creep into my mind.

But the longer I waited, the heavier the silence became.

Chapter 24

Darkness Like a Dream

Steven

Time ticked by, each minute dragging on longer than the last, but I told myself she would walk through the door any moment. Alessandra was always punctual, but tonight, as the minutes slipped away, my heart began to pound with a different kind of anticipation—one tinged with worry.

I glanced at my watch again. She was almost an hour late now. My excitement, which had been bubbling over all day, was slowly being overtaken by a gnawing sense of anxiety. I tried to tell myself that there had to be a good reason. Maybe something came up with her family, or maybe she was stuck in traffic. It wasn't like her to be late without calling, but I clung to the hope that she would walk in any minute, breathless with apologies and explanations.

But when another fifteen minutes passed with no sign of her, my stomach churned. I pulled out my phone, dialing her number with shaky fingers. This time it went straight to an automated message telling me the number was no longer valid. I tried again, and again, each call met with silence.

"Alessandra, where are you?" I murmured under my breath, my voice cracking as I stared at the phone in my hand, willing it to buzz with a reply. But there was nothing —just silence.

The restaurant staff moved quietly around me, clearing away dishes, refilling water glasses that I hadn't touched. I could feel their sympathetic glances, the way they tried not to look at the man sitting alone at the table, waiting for someone who wasn't going to show up.

As the hours dragged on, the hope that had carried me through the day began to crumble, replaced by a sinking dread. This wasn't just a delay. Something was wrong—terribly, horribly wrong. But what? What could have happened to make her miss this night, the night we had been looking forward to for weeks?

By the time I finally stood up, the restaurant was nearly empty, the candles on our table long since extinguished. I left money on the table, murmuring my thanks to the staff as I stumbled out into the cool night air, my heart pounding in my chest.

I tried to call her again as I walked, my footsteps echoing in the deserted streets. Again, nothing. I sent her a text, my hands trembling as I typed out a message that was equal parts worry and desperation.

> Where are you? Are you okay? Please, just let me know you're alright.

But as I hit send, I already knew I wouldn't get a response. *Undelivered.* The silence on the other end was like a black hole, sucking all the light and hope out of me.

When I reached our apartment, the building was dark

and quiet, the kind of silence that felt oppressive, like it was pressing down on my chest. I climbed the stairs two at a time, my heart racing with a mix of fear and hope that maybe—just maybe—she was already here, waiting for me with an explanation that would make everything okay.

But when I opened the door, the sight that greeted me made my blood run cold. The apartment was empty.

Not empty in the sense that she wasn't there. It was empty in the sense that it looked like she had never been there at all.

I stood frozen in the doorway, my eyes sweeping over the room that had once been filled with her things—her books, her clothes, the little trinkets she had collected over the years. All of it was gone. Every trace of her, every sign that she had ever lived here, had been wiped away as if she had never existed.

My breath caught in my throat, my heart hammering against my ribs as I stepped inside, my hands trembling as I reached for the light switch. The harsh light flooded the room, revealing more emptiness—her side of the closet was bare, the drawers that had held her clothes were empty, and the bathroom shelves that had once been crowded with her products were now spotless.

"No," I whispered, stumbling forward as if I could will her things back into existence. I opened the closet, the empty hangers swinging mockingly on the rod. I pulled open the drawers, one by one, only to find them all empty, the scent of her perfume lingering faintly in the air, like a cruel reminder of what was now gone.

My hands shook as I fumbled with my phone, dialing her number once more, praying that this time, she would answer. Being met with silence may as well have been a knife twisting in my chest.

"Alessandra," I choked out, my voice cracking as I sank onto the edge of the bed—the bed we had shared so many nights.

But there was no answer. There was nothing but the cold, empty space around me, the stark reality that she was gone, and I had no idea why.

I don't know how long I sat there, my mind spinning in circles, trying to make sense of the impossible. How could she be gone? How could she just disappear without a word, without any explanation?

We had spent the morning together, snuggled up together after making love before joining my family to celebrate our graduations. We talked about the future and laughed with my family. There had been no sign, no warning that anything was wrong. She had kissed me goodbye, told me she would see me tonight. How could everything change so quickly?

The ring was still in my pocket, a reminder of what I had planned for tonight. I pulled it out, staring at the small velvet box in my hand, the weight of it feeling like a lead weight in my chest. This was supposed to be the night I asked her to be mine forever. But instead, I was left here, alone, with nothing but a broken heart and a thousand unanswered questions.

What had gone wrong? Had I missed something? Had I pushed too hard?

I tried to replay the last few weeks in my mind, searching for clues, for anything that might explain why she would leave me like this. But all I found were memories—moments of laughter, of love, of promises whispered in the dark. How could all of that have been a lie?

As the night wore on, the truth began to sink in, cold and unforgiving. She was gone, and I had no idea if she was ever coming back. I had lost her, and I didn't even know why.

I lay down on the bed, the emptiness swallowing me whole as I stared up at the ceiling, the ring still clutched in my hand. The future I had imagined for us—marriage, a life together, a family—was slipping away, disappearing into the darkness like a dream that had never been real.

And as the tears finally came, hot and unrelenting, I realized that I had never felt so alone in my entire life.

Chapter 25

Irreversible Choices

Alessandra

The day had been perfect, almost like a dream. Standing beside Steven, surrounded by the cheers of our families, the sun shining down on us as we crossed the stage—it felt like everything was finally coming together. But even as I smiled and celebrated with him, the shadow of what I knew was coming loomed over me, dark and unrelenting.

I had tried to ignore it, to push aside the dread that had been gnawing at me for weeks. I wanted to enjoy this day, to savor every moment with Steven, knowing that it might be the last time we were truly happy together. But deep down, I knew it was only a matter of time before reality caught up with me.

After the ceremony, I told Steven I needed to spend some time with my family. It was the truth, but it wasn't the whole truth. He had looked at me with those warm, loving eyes, full of excitement for the evening we had planned, and it took everything in me to smile back, to hide the fear that was twisting my stomach into knots.

"I'll meet you at the restaurant," I had said, forcing my voice to stay steady.

"I can't wait," he'd replied, kissing me softly, his lips lingering on mine like a promise.

As I walked away, the distance between us felt like a chasm, and with every step, I felt the weight of my father's expectations pressing down on me, suffocating in its intensity.

The drive to the estate was a blur, my mind racing with a thousand thoughts, each one more desperate than the last. I had tried to convince myself that I could still find a way out, that I could reason with my father, make him see that Steven was no threat to our family. But deep down, I knew the truth. I knew what he was going to demand of me, and I knew I was powerless to refuse.

When I arrived, the estate was as imposing as ever, the grand facade a cold reminder of the life I could never escape. The guards didn't speak as I passed them, their eyes following me with that same impassive gaze they always had. But I could feel the tension in the air, the way they stood a little straighter, their movements a little sharper. They knew something was coming. They always knew.

My father was waiting for me in his study, the room dimly lit by the fire crackling in the hearth. He didn't look up when I entered, his eyes focused on the glass of whiskey in his hand. The silence stretched out between us, heavy and suffocating, until I couldn't bear it any longer.

"Father," I began, my voice trembling despite my best efforts to stay calm.

He looked up then, his eyes cold and unreadable. "Alessandra."

I swallowed hard, forcing myself to stand tall, even as my knees threatened to buckle. "I know why you've called me here."

"Do you?" he asked, his tone deceptively mild.

I nodded, my throat tightening. "You want me to end things with Steven."

There was a smugness about him I didn't like.

I clenched my fists at my sides, trying to keep my voice steady. "I can't do that. I love him."

His expression didn't change, but the room seemed to grow colder, the air thick with the weight of his authority. "Your love is irrelevant, Alessandra. You were given time to enjoy your little college experience, to play at being a normal girl. But that time is over. You are a Navarra, and it's time you start acting like one."

"I have acted like one," I shot back, my voice sharper than I intended. "I've kept our secrets. I've done everything you've asked of me. But this... This is too much."

He set the glass down on the desk, the soft clink of crystal on wood echoing in the silence. "You were never going to keep him, Alessandra. You knew that from the beginning."

Tears welled in my eyes, but I blinked them back, refusing to let him see me break. "Please, Father, I'm begging you. Let me stay with him. I'll do anything—anything you ask, just don't make me leave him."

For a moment, I thought I saw a flicker of pity in his eyes. But it was gone as quickly as it had appeared, replaced by the cold, calculating gaze I knew so well.

"It's already over, Alessandra." he said, his voice like steel. "All of your things have been moved into your room. And tonight you will prove your loyalty to this family by doing a job that needs to be done."

My heart plummeted, the full weight of his words crashing down on me. "What do you mean?"

"There's a man," he said, leaning back in his chair, his eyes never leaving mine. "Someone who has crossed us one too many times. He needs to be dealt with. And you will do it."

"No," I whispered, shaking my head in disbelief. "I can't... I can't do that."

"You can, and you will," he replied, his tone leaving no room for argument. "If you refuse, Steven will pay the price. You were never going to keep him, Alessandra. But if you want him to live, you will do what I ask."

The room spun around me, my vision blurring as the reality of his words sank in. I was going to lose Steven either way. But if I didn't do what my father demanded, I would lose him in the worst possible way.

"Please, don't do this," I begged, my voice breaking. "There has to be another way."

"There isn't," he said, his tone final. "This is the way it has to be."

I stared at him, my heart shattering into a million pieces. This was it—the end of everything. The life I had dreamed of with Steven, the love we had shared, all of it was being ripped away from me, leaving nothing but a gaping void where my future had once been.

"Fine," I whispered, my voice hollow. "I'll do it. But I want to add on a condition."

His gaze narrowed, suspicion flickering across his features. "What condition?"

I swallowed hard, summoning every ounce of strength I had left. "If I dedicate my life to this family—if I give up Steven and prove my loyalty—you won't arrange a marriage for me. No suitors, no political alliances disguised as engagements. My life will be mine in that respect." I leaned forward, my breath shaking. "If the family needs an heir, I'll take care of that when the time comes. But it will be on my terms. No deals. No forced marriages."

He studied me in silence, his eyes calculating as they searched mine. For a moment, the only sound in the room was the faint ticking of the grandfather clock in the corner. I could feel the weight of the moment pressing down on me, suffocating, as if my entire future rested on this negotiation.

"You want to dictate when and how you produce an heir?" he said finally, his voice as calm as ever, but I could see the tension in his jaw. "You think this family can afford that level of leniency?"

"Yes," I said firmly. "If you trust me to one day lead, then trust me to make that decision. I'll give you everything else. My loyalty, my life. But not that. Not my choice."

He leaned back in his chair, steepling his fingers under his chin while he thought over my request. My pulse raced, but I kept my posture steady, refusing to flinch.

"You understand what you're asking for, don't you?" he said slowly. "No arranged marriage means no immediate alliances. No merging of power through a partner. That will make you vulnerable—make us vulnerable. Are you prepared for that?"

I nodded. "I'll build alliances another way. I don't need a husband to do that."

A long pause followed, and my heart hammered so loudly I was sure he could hear it. Then, finally, he exhaled, the sound heavy. "Fine. No arranged marriage. But if the time comes and you haven't produced an heir, we will revisit this conversation."

"When the time comes, I'll handle it," I said, relief

flooding through me despite the bitterness of the situation. "And you won't interfere."

His eyes locked onto mine, cold and calculating, but after a moment, he nodded. "Agreed."

The word felt like both a victory and a curse. I had bought myself a small piece of freedom, but at what cost?

He stood, signaling that the conversation was over. "You know what you have to do tonight. Don't disappoint me, Alessandra."

I nodded, my throat tight. "I won't."

Without another word, he turned and left the room, leaving me alone with the crushing weight of the deal I had just made.

I had saved myself from one kind of prison, but in doing so, I had trapped myself in another.

The walk to the basement felt like a death march. My legs were heavy, my mind numb as I descended the stairs, the cold air biting at my skin. The basement was dimly lit, the walls lined with concrete, and as I approached the door at the end of the hall, I could hear the faint sounds of someone moving inside.

I paused outside the door, my heart pounding in my chest. My father's words echoed in my mind, reminding me of the consequences if I didn't follow through. But as I reached for the handle, my hand shook so badly I could barely grasp it.

I had never done anything like this before. I had been raised in this world, had known since I was a child that it was brutal, unforgiving. But I had always been shielded from the worst of it, kept at a distance from the violence that sustained our power.

But now, there was no escaping it. No more distance.

No more hiding from the truth of what it meant to be a Navarra.

With a deep breath, I pushed the door open. The man was tied to a chair in the center of the room, his head hanging low. He looked up as I entered, his eyes meeting mine with a mixture of fear and defiance.

I hesitated, my heart pounding in my ears. I could see the fear in his eyes, could feel it radiating off him in waves. This was a man with a family, with a life of his own. And I was about to end it.

"I'm sorry," I whispered, my voice trembling. "I'm so sorry."

But as I moved closer, as I raised the weapon my father had given me, I felt something inside me shatter. The sound of the shot echoed in the small room, loud and final, and I felt the weight of what I had done crash down on me like a tidal wave.

I stood there, frozen, the gun slipping from my fingers as the reality of my actions sank in. I had just taken a life. I had just crossed a line I could never uncross.

My legs gave out, and I sank to the floor, the cold concrete biting into my skin as I stared at the man's lifeless body. I had done this. I had killed him. And there was no going back.

I don't know how long I sat there, numb and shaking, my mind unable to process the enormity of what I had just done. But eventually, I forced myself to stand, to walk back up the stairs, my body moving on autopilot as I made my way out of the basement.

My father was waiting for me at the top of the stairs, his expression unreadable. "It's done?" he asked, his tone flat.

I nodded, my voice gone, my throat raw from holding back the screams that threatened to tear me apart.

"Good," he said, his tone softening slightly. "You did well, Alessandra. I'm proud of you. And Happy Graduation Day, daughter."

His words were like a knife to the heart. I didn't want his pride. I didn't want any of this. All I wanted was Steven, the life we had dreamed of, the love we had shared. But that was gone now, destroyed by my own hand.

I walked to my room without another word, my father's praise ringing hollow in my ears. With each step, I could feel the weight of the decision I had made pressing down on me, suffocating in its finality.

Part Two

The Aftermath

Chapter 26

Leaving Ghosts in the Past

She was gone.

No explanation. No goodbye. Just an empty apartment and a void where our future had once been.

At first, I didn't leave the apartment, thinking she might walk through the door any minute and I needed to be here for that. I needed to be here so she could explain that this was some kind of mistake, a misunderstanding that could be explained with a simple conversation. But as the hours dragged on, hope began to fade, replaced by a gnawing sense of dread. I kept checking my phone, scrolling through old messages, rereading her texts, looking for something—anything—that would tell me where she'd gone.

I scrolled through her texts, reread old messages, and clung to the details like lifelines—but there were no hints, no clues hidden between her words.

I reached out to her friends. They didn't know where she was—or if they did, they weren't saying.

Even Nate tried to help. "You sure you've got the right last name?" he asked after hitting a wall. I could hear the hesitation in his voice, the concern that this was bigger than either of us thought.

I wasn't sure of anything anymore.

I rejected his offer to dig deeper. Alessandra had made me promise not to pry into her family. And for four years, I hadn't. I'd respected her boundaries. I'd believed it didn't matter. But now, that promise felt like a noose tightening around my throat. I kept it anyway.

I spent the third day walking aimlessly through the city. The streets we'd wandered together mocked me with memories—her laughter at a corner café, the bookstore where she'd spent hours browsing. The weight of her absence pressed down on me with every step.

When I got back to the apartment that night, the grief I'd been holding back finally broke free. One minute, I was staring at the empty space where her coffee cup used to sit, and the next, I was on the floor, gasping as tears poured out of me.

I cried until I had nothing left. Not just for her, but for the version of us that had died without warning.

I stayed there, curled up on the floor, my chest hollow and raw. The silence pressed down, thick and suffocating. My breath hitched as I tried to pull myself together, but it wasn't working. The image of her smile, the warmth of her voice, the way she fit perfectly into my arms—it all came rushing back, clawing at me.

How could she leave without saying goodbye? Was she in danger? Was someone keeping her from me?

I told myself she was okay. That she'd had a choice. That she wouldn't just disappear if she wasn't safe. But the fear gnawed at me anyway. What if something had happened to her? What if her world had caught up with her, and I hadn't seen the warning signs?

I wiped my face with the back of my hand and sat up, leaning against the wall. My head throbbed, and the tears had left me exhausted. But something shifted inside me—an ache that wasn't just sadness, but something sharper, more determined.

I told myself it wasn't betrayal driving me. It was closure. If I could understand why she left, maybe I could make peace with it. But deep down, I knew better. I needed to know why. I needed answers

I started piecing things together in my head. The things she'd said over the years that hadn't made sense now demanded my attention. She'd always been guarded about her family. There were no photos, no stories. But she'd mentioned her grandmother's name once—Caterina.

We'd been lying in bed when she told me. "If we ever have a daughter," she'd said softly, her head resting on my chest, "I'd name her Caterina, after my grandmother. She was beautiful and one of the strongest women I've ever known."

I'd smiled then, imagining the family we'd build together. But now that memory burned like acid in my throat. The name that had once been part of our future was now my only clue.

I opened my laptop and searched "Caterina Romano."

Most of the results were irrelevant, but then I saw it:

Caterina Romano Navarra, Beloved Mother and Grandmother, Dies at 78.

I clicked the link.

The obituary's headline barely registered. My focus zeroed in on the photo beneath it.

There she was. Alessandra. Standing by the casket, her young face pale but composed. But the name beneath the photo wasn't Romano—it was Navarra.

Navarra.

I scrolled through the article, my pulse pounding. Caterina Romano had married into the Navarra family, one of the most powerful and notorious crime families in New York. Her son, Lorenzo Navarra, was the current head of the family.

Her father.

I kept reading, my stomach churning. The Navarra family wasn't just rich or powerful—they were dangerous. Their name was tied to rumors of bribes, violence, and disappearances. Business fronts masking criminal enterprises. And Alessandra had grown up in the center of it.

I thought about the fake last name she'd given me: Romano. Her grandmother's maiden name. A shield to protect me from the truth.

The fear I had tried to bury came roaring back. If this was her family—if this was the life she had run from—was she really safe? Or had she been pulled back into something she couldn't escape?

My hands trembled as I scrolled through article after article. I couldn't breathe.

I leaned back in my chair, the weight of it all crashing down. The woman I loved had been living a double life, hiding the truth because her world could have destroyed mine.

I stood and paced down the hallway to the bedroom, my thoughts spiraling. She was out there somewhere—maybe under her family's watch, maybe still running.

What was I supposed to do? Could I track her down somehow? That seemed like a harebrained idea. Based on what I'd just read it sounded a lot like walking straight into a lions' den wearing a steak as a loincloth.

I sat down hard on the bed, my head in my hands, trying

to think through the noise in my brain. My body was exhausted, but my mind refused to slow down. Every time I closed my eyes, I saw her—standing in that photo, distant, unreachable.

What had she been living with all this time? How had she carried the weight of a family like that and never once let me see the cracks?

I raked my hands through my hair, tugging at the roots like the pain could ground me. My phone sat on the nightstand, taunting me. Part of me wanted to call Nate and tell him everything—about the obituary, the Navarras, how terrified I was that something had happened to her and that I wanted to look for her. He'd tell me I was being reckless. He'd try to talk me down.

But that was the problem. I didn't want to be talked down.

I looked around the room we'd shared. The place that had felt like home just a few days ago now felt suffocating, haunted by what had been lost. I'd had to call my family and tell them we broke up—an awkward, painful conversation made worse by the lies I had to tell. Only Nate knew the truth, and even then, I hadn't told him everything.

There was no time to break down again. My new job started in two days. Two days to figure out what I could do before the real world came crashing back in.

I went back to the living room and grabbed my laptop and sat back on the bed. My fingers hovered over the keyboard. What now? I had already gone through everything I could find about the Navarras online. Every article told the same story: powerful, dangerous, untouchable.

If I kept digging, I'd be stepping into a world I wasn't familiar with.

This wasn't some investigation for a school project. This

wasn't a story I could write my way out of. If I got too close, there was no telling what the Navarras would do.

But Alessandra had lived in that world her whole life. She knew its rules. She'd left to protect me, but she'd also left to protect herself.

Maybe that meant she had a plan.

I scrolled through my search history, retracing my steps. What was I doing? I had no plan, no real direction. Just a gut feeling that I couldn't shake. If I went looking for her, I'd be risking everything. And even if I found her, what would I say? Would she even want me there, or had she made her decision and moved on?

But the alternative—doing nothing—felt like drowning.

I thought about the engagement ring still sitting in the drawer by the bed, the one I'd planned to give her after graduation. I could see it so clearly: her face lighting up, the way she'd laugh through her tears as she said yes. We were supposed to be celebrating right now. Making love. Planning a wedding. Not this.

I stood up and opened the drawer, taking the ring out of its box. It was cold in my hand, the weight of it heavier than it should have been. I traced the band with my thumb, imagining the life we were supposed to have. Now, it sat here like a reminder of everything I couldn't fix.

My throat tightened, and I slipped the ring back into the drawer, shutting it softly like closing a door on a dream. But I couldn't close the door on her. Not yet.

I grabbed my phone and scrolled through my contacts until I found Mitch's name. My hand hovered over it for a moment before I pressed the call button.

He picked up on the third ring.

"Steven? You okay?"

"No," I said honestly.

His voice softened. "I figured. What's going on?"

I didn't give him all the details. I just sat there, listening to his voice, the comfort of having someone on the other end of the line reminding me that I wasn't completely alone.

When we hung up, I set my phone on the nightstand. As I did, the screen lit up, and I caught a glimpse of my lock screen—the picture of Alessandra and me on the beach last summer, laughing, her arm draped around my neck like we had all the time in the world.

The ache in my chest tightened, and on impulse, I opened her social media profile.

It was gone.

Her accounts had been deleted within the last couple of hours.

I stared at the blank page, my heart thudding in my chest.

I set the phone down and leaned forward, resting my elbows on my knees. My breath felt shallow, like I was drowning in the weight of it all.

If she didn't want to be found, maybe I'd never find her.

That didn't mean I was giving up on the idea. I just had to go about it the right way. I just wasn't sure what that was, yet.

Chapter 27

Self Sacrifice

Alessandra

The weeks following graduation night passed in a blur. Time seemed to lose all meaning, each day bleeding into the next as I went through the motions of my new life. The life I had chosen—no, the life I had been forced into. The life I had accepted, with all its cruelty and coldness.

I had done what my father asked. I had proven my loyalty, committed the act that now tethered me irrevocably to the Navarra family, to the world I had spent so long wanting to escape. But in doing so, I had destroyed something far more precious: my chance at forever with Steven. The life we could have had, the happiness I had once dared to dream of—it was all gone, shattered by the echo of a single gunshot.

The man's face haunted me. His eyes, wide with fear, the way he had looked at me as I pulled the trigger. I could still feel the weight of the gun in my hand, the way it had trembled as I tried to steady myself, the deafening sound that had followed, and the awful, awful silence that came after.

I had done it for Steven. That was the only way I could make sense of it, the only way I could justify the blood on my hands. I had killed a man, but I had saved the man I loved. I had kept him safe, protected him from a world he could never understand. But that protection came at a price —a price that was too high, a price that had cost me everything.

I hadn't seen Steven since that day. I knew that by now, he would have realized I wasn't coming back. He would have found the empty apartment, the shell of a life we had once shared. He would have questions—questions I could never answer.

The first few days after the event, I had numbed myself, shutting down every emotion, every thought that threatened to break through the fragile barriers I had started to rebuild around my heart. It was the only way to survive, to keep moving forward without collapsing under the weight of what I had done. But no matter how hard I tried, the memories crept in, the guilt gnawing at me like a persistent, ravenous beast.

I spent hours alone in my room, staring at the walls, the ceiling, anything to keep my mind from wandering. But it was impossible. Every time I closed my eyes, I saw him—Steven. His smile, his laughter, the way he had looked at me that last morning, full of love and hope. And then the man in the basement, the life I had taken in cold blood.

If my tears had been counted since then, they'd probably outnumber the raindrops currently falling outside.

The people around me had noticed the change. How could they not? They had to have noticed how I had withdrawn, how I had become quieter, more reserved. But no one dared to question it. No one in this world ever did. They saw the coldness, the distance in my eyes, and they mistook it for strength, for the ruthless determination my father had always wanted me to have. But they didn't see the truth. They didn't see the brokenness that lay beneath, the emptiness that had settled deep in my chest, suffocating in its intensity.

My father, of course, was pleased. I had proven myself to him, shown him that I was capable of doing whatever was necessary to protect the family. He had praised me, congratulated me on a job well done, but his words had rung hollow in my ears. I didn't want his approval. I didn't want any of this. All I wanted was the life I had lost, the love I had sacrificed for a future that now felt meaningless.

I was trapped, bound by blood and loyalty to a family that had never truly been mine. The life I had dreamed of, the life I had dared to hope for, was gone. And in its place was a cold, empty existence, one that I had chosen—no, one that had been forced upon me, one I had been born into and could never escape.

I had tried to find solace in the idea that I had saved Steven, that he was safe and far away from this world. But even that comfort was fleeting, tainted by the knowledge that I had hurt him, that I had abandoned him without a word, leaving him to wonder what had gone wrong, why I had left.

The memories of our time together played on a loop in my mind—the laughter, the quiet moments, the promises we had made to each other. How happy we'd been when we were together. But now, those memories were laced with a bitter edge, a reminder of everything I had given up, everything I had lost. The more I thought about him, the more the sadness grew, the more the emptiness inside me expanded, threatening to swallow me whole.

The world outside my room continued to turn, the people around me continued to live their lives, but I felt disconnected from it all, as if I were living in a different reality, one that was cold and colorless. My father had given me what I wanted—a way out of an arranged marriage, a promise that I could continue to serve the family without the chains of a husband. But even that victory felt hollow, meaningless in the face of everything else I had lost.

I didn't know how to move forward. I didn't know how to live with what I had done, with the choices I had made. All I knew was that I had to keep going, keep pretending, keep living the life my father expected of me. But inside, I was dying, slowly, piece by piece, as the weight of my actions crushed me.

There was no way out. No escape from the obligations I had been born into, no chance for the life I had once dreamed of. All I had left was this—this cold, empty existence, this life of duty and loyalty to a family that had stolen everything from me.

As I lay in my bed that night, staring up at the ceiling, I felt nothing . The tears had dried up, the sadness turned to a dull ache, and all that was left were beautiful haunting memories. I had made my choice. I had sacrificed everything for Steven's safety, for the family's approval. But in doing so, I had lost myself.

And as the darkness closed in around me, I realized that there was no going back. This was my life now. This was who I had become. And I would have to live with that.

Chapter 28

Seeds of Doubt

Alessandra

I dove headfirst into the family business under my father's watchful eye. Every day was a test, a challenge to prove that I belonged here—that I wasn't just Lorenzo Navarra's daughter but a leader in my own right.

Eventually, I'd be the leader, the *donna*. It was my birthright. Even now, the weight of my responsibilities pressed down on me, heavier than anything I had carried before. I was no longer the girl who had left this world behind to pursue a normal life. I was stepping into the role I was born for, and I had no choice but to embrace it.

I'd already been involved in more operations than I could count. I had witnessed the brutal efficiency of the Navarra family's dealings, learned the intricacies of our alliances and rivalries, and discovered just how delicate the balance of power truly was. But there was a part of me that still felt like an outsider, still felt the need to prove myself, not just to my father, but to everyone who served him.

It wasn't that they doubted my intelligence or my capabilities. No, they respected me enough—at least outwardly. But I could feel it in the way they looked at me, in the way they sometimes hesitated before following my orders. They were waiting to see if I could handle the pressure, if I could be as ruthless and decisive as my father. And I was determined not to disappoint them.

But there was one man whose respect I hadn't yet earned, one man whose loyalty was more to my father than to me—Marco, my father's consigliere. He had been by my father's side for as long as I could remember, a constant presence in the shadows, advising, guiding, and sometimes leading the family's operations. He was respected, feared even, by everyone in our world. But now, with me stepping into a leadership role, I could sense a shift in his demeanor, a subtle undercurrent of doubt and resistance.

Marco was loyal to my father, no question about that. But that loyalty didn't necessarily extend to me. And that was something I couldn't afford to ignore.

Tonight's meeting was going to be crucial. We were planning a major operation in Brooklyn, one that would send a clear message to the de Luca family and anyone else who dared to challenge us. It was a delicate operation, one that required precision and a well-thought-out strategy. I had spent hours going over every detail, ensuring that nothing was left to chance. But I knew that this meeting would be the true test—whether the lieutenants would trust my plan or if they would look to Marco for guidance.

As I approached the meeting room, I took a deep breath, steeling myself for what was to come. The door loomed before me, heavy and imposing, a gateway to the world I was now fully immersed in. I reached for the handle, my fingers brushing against the cool metal, and pushed it open.

The room was thick with tension as I entered, the

murmurs of the soldiers silencing the moment they saw me. My heels clicked against the marble floor, each step echoing through the expansive meeting room. They were all here—the most powerful men in the Navarra family, and they were waiting for me to take control or fail.

I reached the head of the table, the seat that had always been reserved for my father, and placed my hands on the cool surface. My eyes swept over the faces before me, noting the mix of respect, wariness, and—yes—doubt in their eyes. They weren't used to taking orders from me, not yet. But that was about to change.

"There's a situation," I began, my voice cutting through the silence like a blade. "The de Luca family is planning a move against us. They've grown bold, thinking we're vulnerable. That ends today."

I could see the ripple of unease pass through the room, the men exchanging glances. Good. Let them be uncomfortable. Let them understand the gravity of the situation.

"We need to act quickly and decisively," I continued, leaning forward slightly, my gaze locked on each of them in turn. "This is not just about defense; it's about sending a message. We don't just survive—we dominate."

Marco sat beside my father, his expression unreadable. I could feel his eyes on me, assessing, evaluating, waiting for me to make a mistake. He had always been a master of control, never revealing more than he intended, and tonight was no different.

As I outlined the plan, I could see the gears turning in Marco's mind. His posture was relaxed, but I knew better than to be fooled by it. Marco was like a coiled viper, always ready to strike.

"We'll target their operations in Brooklyn," I said, tracing the map on the table with my finger. "We'll hit them hard, but we'll be smart about it. We can't afford any collateral damage—it needs to be clean and precise."

The older lieutenants nodded, their eyes following my every move. But Marco remained silent, his gaze never leaving me. I could feel the weight of his scrutiny, the unspoken challenge hanging in the air.

Finally, Marco cleared his throat, breaking the silence. "With all due respect, Miss Navarra, I disagree." His voice was calm, measured, but the edge in his tone was unmistakable. "If we want to send a message, it shouldn't be subtle. We need to make them bleed publicly. Set their warehouses on fire. Take out key lieutenants where it hurts. Leave them scrambling to recover."

I narrowed my eyes. "A chaotic strike like that is messy, Marco. It's unpredictable, and it risks pulling civilians into the crossfire. We'd gain short-term intimidation, but we'd lose long-term stability. If we do it my way, we may not only exert power, but take control of their current operation. If it looks beneficial, we'll keep it. If not, we dismantle it and continue to show everyone that we don't need what we take. We take what we want."

He shrugged, his lips curving into a faint smirk. "Stability isn't the point here. Fear is. The de Lucas thrive on public perception. If we burn one of their strongholds to the ground in broad daylight, no one will question our dominance."

"Except the NYPD," I shot back, keeping my tone sharp. "And every rival family waiting for us to slip up. A public assault could bring heat down on all of us. We're not just playing offense here—we're protecting the family."

Marco leaned back in his chair, folding his hands in front of him. "You're worried about the fallout. I'm worried about whether they'll be too afraid to hit us again. A strike in the shadows might send a message, but a spectacle will make sure they never forget it."

My father, who had been silent until now, finally spoke. "There's merit in both approaches," he said, his voice measured. "Alessandra's plan is sound, but Marco raises a valid point. We can't afford to be seen as weak."

I nodded, acknowledging my father's input, but I could feel the sting of his words. He was trying to strike a balance, to placate both me and Marco, but I couldn't shake the feeling that he was subtly questioning my judgment.

"This isn't about hesitation," I said, my voice firm. "It's about strategy. We're not just sending a message to the de Lucas—we're sending a message to everyone. We need to show that we're not just strong, but smart. That we're in control."

Marco studied me for a moment, his expression unreadable. Then, slowly, he nodded. "Very well. But we should be prepared for any retaliation. The de Lucas won't take this lying down."

"I'm counting on it," I replied, holding his gaze. "But by the time they realize what's happened, it'll be too late."

The room fell silent again, the tension thick in the air. My father's eyes flicked between me and Marco, as if weighing his own thoughts on the matter. Finally, he nodded, a gesture of approval that was as much for me as it was for Marco.

"We move forward with the plan," my father said, his voice carrying the weight of authority. "Alessandra will lead the operation. Marco, make sure everything is in place."

There was a chorus of agreement from the lieutenants, but I could sense the underlying tension. Marco's challenge had been subtle, but it was there, a seed of doubt that had been planted in the minds of the others. I couldn't afford to let it grow.

As the meeting concluded, I lingered behind, watching as the men filtered out of the room. Marco was one of the last to leave, his expression unreadable as he passed by me. I knew I couldn't let this simmering tension go unchecked.

"Marco," I called after him, my voice steady. He paused, turning to face me. "I'd like to speak with you. In private."

He nodded, following me as I led him down one of the quieter hallways of the estate. The walls were lined with portraits of my ancestors, their stern faces a reminder of the legacy I was now a part of. We stopped in a secluded corner, away from prying eyes and ears.

"Do you have a problem with my leadership?" I asked, my tone direct.

Marco raised an eyebrow, clearly surprised by my question. "I'm only looking out for the family, Alessandra. Your father has always trusted me to do what's best, and I'm simply continuing that tradition."

"Continuing that tradition?" I repeated, my voice laced with skepticism. "Or are you questioning whether I'm fit to lead? Because if you remember, I didn't ask for this. My father put me in this position."

Marco's expression didn't change, but there was a flicker of something unsettling in his eyes. "I'm not questioning you," he said smoothly. "I'm offering advice. You're new to this role, and I have years of experience. I'd be remiss if I didn't share my insights."

"Insights or doubts?" I shot back, crossing my arms over my chest. "You've been at my father's side for years, Marco, and I respect that. But don't mistake my respect for weakness. I've been given this responsibility because my father trusts me to do the job."

"For now," Marco replied evenly. "But trust is earned, not given freely. If you want to lead this family, you'll have to prove that you're capable of making the tough decisions."

"I've made plenty of tough decisions already," I retorted, refusing to back down. "And I'm prepared to make more. But let me be clear, Marco—if you're not with me, then you're against me. And being against me is going against the family. I don't want anyone in my corner who isn't fully committed to this family's success."

For a moment, the air between us crackled with unspoken tension. "I've always been loyal to the Navarras," he said, his voice low. "And just like trust, loyalty is also earned, not given."

The implication was clear, and it hit me like a punch to the gut. Marco didn't see me as his leader—not yet, maybe not ever. He still saw me as Lorenzo's daughter, not as the head of the Navarra family. But I couldn't let him see how deeply his words had cut.

"You're right," I said, my tone cold. "Loyalty is earned, and I intend to prove that I deserve it. That being said, if you can't stand by me, you're in my way. You should know that I won't tolerate anything or anyone that could undermine the family."

Marco didn't flinch, his expression remaining stoic. His voice, however, was a low growl when he said, "I've always done what's best for the Navarras, and I'll continue to do so. But don't mistake my loyalty for blind obedience. I'll speak up when I believe it's necessary."

I held his stare, accepting his words for what they were—a warning. My last words to him were like ice. "Just remember who's in charge."

With that, I turned and walked away, my heart pounding in my chest. The conversation had gone exactly as I had expected, but it didn't make it any easier to swallow. Marco wasn't fully on my side, and that meant I had to be more vigilant than ever.

As I walked back to my quarters, I couldn't shake the feeling that Marco's subtle defiance was just the beginning. There would be others who doubted me, others who questioned my ability to lead. But I couldn't afford to let those doubts undermine me. I had to be stronger, smarter, and more ruthless than anyone expected.

When I reached my room, I closed the door behind me, leaning against it for a moment as I gathered my thoughts. The weight of leadership was heavy, but I had no choice but to bear it. This was my family, my legacy, and I would do whatever it took to protect it.

But as I stared out the window at the darkening sky, I realized that the biggest challenge I would face might not come from outside threats, but from within.

I knew I couldn't trust Marco fully, but I also knew I couldn't afford to alienate him. I would have to play this carefully, bide my time, and wait for the right moment to assert my authority. He was a potential threat, but he was also a valuable asset—one that I couldn't afford to lose until I was fully in control.

As I stood there, staring out at the darkening horizon, I made a silent vow to myself. I would earn Marco's loyalty, or I would find a way to neutralize him. Either way, I would secure my place as the future leader of this family. No matter what it took.

And if that meant making some difficult decisions along the way, then so be it.

Chapter 29

Running from Myself

Steven

I had accepted the position at an online magazine months before graduation, a step forward in my career that would allow me to stay in New York while still chasing the stories that mattered. It was supposed to be the perfect balance—building my future with Alessandra while advancing as a journalist in one of the most exciting cities in the world. But now, almost a year later, that vision was shattered, and continuing to stay in a place that held so many memories of her had become unbearable.

I'd spent every moment I wasn't working searching online or roaming the streets of New York, hoping to catch a glimpse of her. Dead ends became motivation that turned into obsession until one day I realized I was chasing shadows. She was gone, and I was tearing myself apart looking for someone who didn't want to be found.

The magazine's headquarters were right in Manhattan, just a few subway stops away from the apartment we'd shared. Before, I had imagined myself commuting from our home, grabbing coffee on the way, and returning home to her smile at the end of the day. Now, all of those dreams felt like nightmares.

I couldn't do it. I couldn't stay in New York, not with the ghost of her lingering in every corner, not with the knowledge that she had left me behind without a word. The city, once filled with promise and excitement, now felt like a prison, its streets and buildings a constant reminder of everything I had lost.

So, I made a decision. I would take the first available assignment, wherever it was, however dangerous. I needed to get out, to put as much distance between myself and this city as possible. When I called my editor, he didn't hesitate to offer me a spot on their international investigative team—a position that would take me far from New York and deep into some of the world's most perilous places.

Before I left, I made one last trip home to say goodbye to my parents and brothers.

My mom knew something was wrong—she always did—but I couldn't bring myself to tell her the truth. I just hugged her a little tighter, promising that I'd call as often as I could.

My dad, doing better than he had been in a long time, gave me a firm handshake, his eyes filled with pride and concern.

And my brothers—Nate, always the protector, and Mitch, always the jokester—both offered their own versions of support.

"You'll be back before we know it," Nate said, clapping a hand on my shoulder. There was an unspoken understanding in his eyes, a knowledge that I needed to do this, to find my own way through the pain.

"Just stay alive," Mitch added with a grin, trying to

lighten the mood. But I could see the worry in his eyes. He looked at me as if he wasn't sure I'd come back the same. We'd seen it happen with Nate when he came home from the Marines. Thankfully, he'd found a good woman, a good therapist, and a job that filled the needs of his adrenaline junkie side.

I left them with promises I wasn't sure I could keep and headed straight for the airport.

My first major assignment took me deep into the jungles of South America, where drug trafficking networks ruled with an iron fist. I was tasked with uncovering the truth behind a series of brutal massacres in small, isolated villages—massacres that the local government claimed were the work of rival cartels, but which locals whispered had far more sinister origins.

The journey was grueling. After a long flight, I'd found myself in a small, dilapidated airport, where the oppressive heat clung to my skin like a wet blanket. From there, I'd boarded a rusted-out jeep driven by a local guide who spoke little English. We drove for hours on rough, unpaved roads, the dense jungle pressing in on all sides. The deeper we went, the more I realized how far from civilization I truly was.

My guide, a wiry man named Luis, was a wealth of information. Though his English was broken, he spoke with a quiet intensity that made me pay attention. He told me about the villages we passed—places that had been abandoned for years, their people either killed or driven away by the cartels. He pointed out the remnants of a village that had been burned to the ground, its charred skeletons standing as a testament to the violence that plagued the region.

"There is no law here," Luis said, his voice grim. "Only

the law of the jungle. The strong survive, the weak... they disappear."

As we neared our destination, Luis became more cautious, his eyes constantly scanning the jungle around us. We were entering cartel territory, a place where outsiders were not welcome. I could see the tension in his shoulders, the way his hands tightened on the steering wheel. But he never hesitated, never wavered in his determination to get me where I needed to go.

Finally, we arrived at a small, remote village nestled in the heart of the jungle. The air was thick with the scent of damp earth and rotting vegetation, the sounds of the jungle a constant backdrop to the quiet murmurs of the villagers. They watched me with wary eyes as I stepped out of the jeep, their faces etched with suspicion and fear.

Luis spoke to them in rapid Spanish, introducing me as a journalist from the United States. There was a moment of silence, then a woman stepped forward—a matriarch of sorts, her face lined with age and hardship. She studied me for a long moment, her eyes searching, before she finally nodded.

"You want to know the truth," she said, her voice low and steady. "Then you must see it for yourself."

She led me through the village, past simple huts made of wood and thatch, to a clearing where the earth was disturbed, the ground still raw and uneven. I didn't need to ask what it was—I knew a mass grave when I saw one.

"This is what they do," she said, her voice tinged with bitterness. "They come in the night, like shadows. They take our men, our sons, and leave us with nothing but death."

Her words hung heavy in the air, the weight of them pressing down on me. I could feel the eyes of the villagers on me, could sense their desperation, their fear. They wanted someone to tell their story, to expose the horrors they had endured. And I knew that I was their only hope.

Over the next several days, I immersed myself in their world, documenting their stories, their pain. I traveled to other villages, each one with its own tale of terror and loss. I spoke to survivors, to those who had lost everything, and to those who had risked their lives to fight back against the cartels. Each story was more harrowing than the last, a testament to the brutality that had become a part of daily life in this forgotten corner of the world.

But it wasn't just the cartels that were responsible for the atrocities. The deeper I dug, the more I uncovered a web of corruption that stretched far beyond the jungles. Government officials, military leaders, even multinational corporations were complicit in the violence, their greed and ambition fueling the fires of conflict.

As I pieced together the puzzle, the story took shape—a story that would expose the truth, that would shine a light on the darkness that had engulfed these people for so long. It was a story that needed to be told, and I was determined to be the one to tell it.

But as the days turned into weeks, and the weeks into months, I began to realize that no matter how far I ran, no matter how deep I buried myself in my work, I couldn't escape the memories of Alessandra. She was always there, lurking in the corners of my mind, a constant reminder of the life I had left behind.

The jungle was a harsh, unforgiving place, but it was nothing compared to the emptiness I felt inside. The work was a temporary distraction, a way to keep the pain at bay, but it could never fill the void she had left behind.

My reputation as a hard-hitting investigative journalist

grew as I tackled stories in war zones, corrupt governments, and criminal underworlds. The more perilous the assignment, the more eagerly I accepted it. Danger was a distraction, a way to forget the ache that Alessandra had left behind.

In the end, I knew that I could spend the rest of my life chasing stories, uncovering the darkest secrets of the world, but it would never be enough. Because the truth was, I wasn't just running from the memories—I was running from myself, and I knew it.

Chapter 30

An Heiress of Power

Alessandra

Two years had passed since I walked away from the life I had wanted so desperately to make my own. The girl who once dreamt of a different future died that night, replaced by someone harder, sharper—a woman shaped by the cold realities of the world she was born into. I had learned to embrace that world, to master it, because there was no other choice. The life I lived now demanded nothing less than complete devotion and utter compromise of the woman I once was.

The estate was alive with activity as I walked through its grand halls, the air buzzing with the kind of tension that came with significant power moves. Today was a crucial day, the op one that would be a big step for the family, and I could feel the weight of it pressing down on me. I wasn't just an observer anymore, I was a player—an important one. My father had made that clear.

The meeting room was filled with the heavy scent of cigars and the murmurs of low voices. My father's most trusted men were already seated around the long table, their faces a mix of anticipation and calculation. As I entered, all eyes turned to me, and for a moment, I felt the familiar surge of unease—the remnants of the girl I used to be wanting to take point and lead me right back out of the room. But I buried that part of me deep, as I had learned to do, and took my place at the table beside my father.

"Alessandra," he greeted me with a nod, his voice carrying the authority that had kept our family at the top for so long. "We have important matters to discuss."

I nodded in return, my expression as unreadable as his. I had become a master at hiding my emotions, at presenting only what was necessary. It was a skill that had served me well, one I had honed through countless hours of practice. Today would be no different.

The discussions were intense, each decision carrying the potential to shift the balance of power in our favor—or against us. Expansion, alliances, territory—it was all on the table, and I was no longer ignorant nor was I a passive participant. My father had begun to trust me with more responsibility, to value my input, and I wasn't about to let him down.

As the conversation turned to securing new alliances, I spoke up, my voice steady and confident. "The Benedetto family has been pressing into our territory for months. We need to either bring them to the table or push them back before they become a larger problem."

Several heads nodded in agreement, but my father's gaze remained fixed on me, appraising. "And how do you suggest we handle it?"

I met his gaze without flinching. "We bring them in for a meeting, offer them a deal that benefits both sides. But we make it clear that any move against us will be met with swift and decisive action."

It was a delicate balance—showing strength without overstepping—but it was one I had learned to navigate well. My father's expression didn't change, but I could see the approval in his eyes.

"Very well," he said, turning to his right-hand man. "Make the arrangements."

The meeting continued, with more discussions and decisions that would shape the future of our operations. I remained engaged, contributing when necessary, always careful to gauge the reactions of those around me. These men had spent their lives in this world, and they respected power. I had earned some of that respect, but it was a tenuous thing—one wrong move, one sign of weakness, and it could all come crashing down.

When the meeting finally ended, my father pulled me aside, his expression unreadable. "There's a negotiation that needs handling," he said, his tone leaving no room for refusal. "I want you to take care of it."

I nodded, already anticipating the challenge ahead. The Navarra name carried weight, but it also came with expectations—expectations that I had to meet, no matter the cost. "Consider it done."

The negotiation was with a smaller family, one that had been trying to make inroads into our territory. They were ambitious, but they lacked the resources and connections to challenge us outright. It was a delicate situation—one that required both finesse and a show of strength.

I arrived at the meeting location with my father's words echoing in my mind. There were no mistakes allowed in this world, no second chances. I had to be perfect, had to prove that I was worthy of the trust he had placed in me. As the alternative was permanent silence in most cases, I could be perfect.

The negotiation went smoothly, my words measured, my tone calm but firm. I knew the stakes, and I wasn't about to let anything slip through my fingers. By the end of it, the other family had agreed to our terms, their leader shaking my hand with a mix of respect and wariness. They knew who I was, what I represented, and that was enough to keep them in line.

As I left the meeting, a small part of me felt a flicker of satisfaction. I had done it—again. I had proven my worth, had reinforced my place in this world. But the satisfaction was fleeting, quickly replaced by the hollow emptiness that had become all too familiar.

I drove back to the estate, my mind wandering despite my best efforts to keep it focused. It was dangerous to let my thoughts drift, to allow myself to reflect on the choices I had made, the life I was living. But some days, like today, it was impossible to avoid.

My father had been dropping hints about potential suitors for months, seeing it as another way to secure alliances, to strengthen our position. But I had resisted, reminding him of our deal and convincing him that I was more valuable unencumbered, that my independence was an asset to the family. He relented, but I knew it was only a matter of time before he pressed the issue again.

Marriage—love—those were distant, alien concepts now. They belonged to a different life, a life that had ended the moment I walked away from Steven. I had buried that part of myself, had forced myself to forget, to move on. But some days, like today, it was harder to keep the memories at bay.

As I pulled into the driveway of the estate, I allowed

myself a brief moment to think about him. Steven. The name was like a knife to the heart, sharp and painful. I hadn't let myself think about him in months, hadn't allowed myself to feel the weight of what I had lost. But today, the memory of him was too strong, too overwhelming to ignore.

I had loved him. Truly, deeply loved him. And in a different life, we might have had a future together. But that life could never exist, and all that remained was the shadow of the woman I used to be. A shadow that had grown darker, colder, more ruthless with each passing day.

I pushed the thoughts aside as I walked into the estate, forcing myself to focus on the present, on the life I had chosen. There was no room for weakness here, no room for regret. I had made my choices, and I had to live with them.

But as I climbed the stairs to my room, the emptiness lingered, gnawing at the edges of my consciousness. It was a void that nothing could fill, a reminder of the soul I had lost when I turned my back on the only man I had ever truly loved.

I reached my room and closed the door behind me, leaning against it for a moment as I tried to steady my breath. This was my life now—cold, calculated, and empty. I was a Navarra, an heir to a legacy of power and blood. And I had become everything my father wanted me to be.

But at what cost?

I walked to the window and looked out at the sprawling estate, the manicured gardens, the guards patrolling the grounds. This was my world now, a world I had been born into, a world I had fought to survive in. And I had succeeded. I had become everything my father had trained me to be.

As I stood there, the weight of my choices bore down, threatening to crush me. When the pressure became overwhelming, I turned away from the window and crossed the room. I slipped off my shoes and sank onto the bed, the familiar luxury of the sheets doing little to comfort me. Lying there, I stared up at the ceiling, the emptiness of the room closing in like a vice.

I squeezed my eyes shut, but that only made it worse. The memories I constantly fought to bury pushed their way forward, relentless and unbidden. Memories I only allowed myself in moments of weakness—moments like this, when every choice I had ever made threatened to haunt me.

I could feel the warmth of Steven's hand in mine, hear his laughter, see the way his eyes crinkled at the corners when he smiled at me like I was the center of his world. My breath caught as the memory shifted, and suddenly I was back in our apartment, lying in his arms, the sound of rain pattering softly against the window.

His voice had been low, almost sleepy, when he whispered, "Stay. Stay with me forever."

And I had smiled through the tears I hadn't let him see. "Forever sounds nice."

Even then, I had known forever wasn't ours to have.

The ache inside me deepened as the memory wrapped tighter around me. I pulled the pillow closer, clutching it to my chest, as if it could anchor me to something real. My body trembled with longing, with grief, with the hollow emptiness of knowing that what I wanted most was already lost.

His name slipped from my lips in a broken whisper, and the tears came hot and fast. I curled onto my side, pressing my face into the pillow, ashamed of how desperate I was for even the memory of him. The illusion had carried me for a fleeting moment, but now it was gone—leaving nothing but the raw, unbearable truth.

I missed him. I wanted him.

I had no right to feel this way. No right to want him when I had been the one to leave.

The guilt gnawed at me, burrowing deep, but it couldn't fill the void left by the loss of him. The warmth of release had been a lie, a fleeting comfort that only made the ache sharper now that it was gone.

I wiped my eyes, my breath still ragged as I stared at the ceiling, the shadows shifting as moonlight filtered through the curtains. Steven was my past. I had told myself that over and over again, trying to believe it. But nights like this proved otherwise.

I forced myself to sit up, the cooled air biting against my damp skin. My reflection in the mirror across the room looked foreign to me—flushed cheeks, tear-streaked eyes, and a hollow stare that didn't belong to the woman I had become. The woman who was supposed to be strong, in control, untouchable.

With a shaky breath, I stood, righting my clothes and pulling the covers over the bed as if erasing the evidence of my weakness could erase it. I walked to the window, pressing my forehead against the cool glass, hoping the cold would numb the lingering desire and shame.

My chest ached with a longing I had no right to feel. I had chosen this life. I had walked away.

But knowing that didn't make it hurt any less.

I stayed there for a while, letting the chill seep into my skin, as if punishing myself for the pleasure I had stolen from a memory. The estate grounds stretched out before me, the manicured gardens and patrolling guards a reminder of the world I was bound to—a world that didn't have room for love or regret.

Tomorrow, I would bury this part of myself again,

locking it away where it couldn't weaken me. Tomorrow, I would be the Alessandra my father needed me to be. But tonight, with the weight of the memory still clinging to me, I allowed myself this moment of vulnerability.

Just tonight.

Then, I would forget him all over again.

Chapter 31

The Iron Grip

Alessandra

The room was thick with tension as I entered, the murmurs of the soldiers silencing the moment they saw me. They were all here—the most powerful men in the Navarra family, and they were waiting for me.

I reached the head of the table, the seat that had always been reserved for my father, and placed my hands on the cool surface. My eyes swept over the faces before me, noting the mix of respect, wariness, and—yes—doubt in their eyes. They still weren't used to taking orders from me, not yet. But that was about to change.

"There's a situation," I began, my voice cutting through the silence like a blade. "There are rumblings that the Valenti family is planning a move against us. They've grown bold, thinking we're vulnerable. That ends today."

The Valenti family had always been a threat, second only to us in power, influence, and reach across the city. For years, they had operated just beneath us, strong enough to be respected but never bold enough to challenge the Navarras directly. Until now.

I could see the ripple of unease pass through the room, the men exchanging glances. Good. Let them be uncomfortable. Let them understand the gravity of the situation.

"We need to act quickly and decisively," I continued, leaning forward slightly, my gaze locked on each of them in turn. "This is not just about defense; it's about sending a message. We don't just survive—we dominate."

Marco shifted in his seat, leaning forward slightly. "Miss Navarra, with all due respect, wouldn't it be wise to wait for your father to return before making any bold moves? His presence—"

I cut him off before he could finish. "My father entrusted me with this operation for a reason. He's taking time to recover, and in the meantime, I'm leading."

It had only been a few weeks since his heart attack—one that could have killed him if Nico hadn't been there to act quickly. The doctors insisted he step back from day-to-day operations, but even that had sent shockwaves through the organization. My father had always been the family's anchor, a force of nature. Without him in his seat, people like Marco saw an opening, and rivals like the Valentis grew bold.

But this was no time to dwell on what had already happened. I held Marco's gaze, daring him to challenge me further. "Unless you want to send a message to our enemies that the Navarras are vulnerable, I suggest you stop questioning his decision."

The room fell silent, the weight of my words sinking in. Marco sat back, his lips pressed into a thin line, but he didn't argue further. I saw the flicker of something in his eyes—perhaps respect, perhaps fear. It didn't matter. What mattered was that he, and everyone else in the room, understood that I was in charge.

I finally took a seat in the large ornate leather back chair.

"I've already made the necessary arrangements," I continued, addressing the rest of the room. "We'll strike their operations in Brooklyn tonight. I want it done cleanly, efficiently, and with a clear message: no one challenges the Navarras and lives to talk about it."

There was a moment of silence, the weight of my words sinking in. Then, one by one, they nodded, acknowledging my command. This was my moment, and I seized it with both hands.

"I'll lead the operation myself," I said, straightening up. "And I expect each of you to play your part. Failure is not an option."

The scent of expensive cigars and aged whiskey, a hallmark of every high-level meeting in the underworld, permeated the air. The leather of the chair was cool against my back as I surveyed the faces around me. Men who had sworn their loyalty to the Navarra name, men who had killed and bled for the family. Tonight, they would follow me into the lion's den, and I needed them to trust that I could lead them out.

"Nico," I said, my voice low but commanding. "What's the latest?"

Nico leaned forward, his sharp eyes gleaming in the dim light. "The Valenti deal is set for tonight. Midnight. A shipment of arms, but that's not the real prize. They've got a representative from the Giordano family coming in. If the Valentis secure their support, it could shift the balance of power in their favor."

I nodded, absorbing the information. The Valentis were

always a problem, but if they managed to ally with the Giordanos, they would become a threat we couldn't ignore. This wasn't just about a shipment; it was about the future of the family, our survival in a world that didn't tolerate weakness.

"Have the Giordanos been paid?" I asked, leaning back in my chair, my fingers tapping rhythmically on the armrest.

"Not yet," Nico replied, a slight smile tugging at the corner of his mouth. "And that's where we come in."

I met his gaze, understanding the unspoken plan. We weren't going to fight the Valentis head-on; we were going to undermine them, strip away their allies until they had nothing left. And we'd do it slowly and methodically so they didn't know what was happening until they were at the bottom of the barrel trying to claw their way back out.

The Giordanos were only loyal to money and power—two things the Navarra family could provide in abundance. The outcome of this operation was clenched before it began in my mind.

I turned to the others at the table, my voice steely. "Tonight, we're not just disrupting a deal. We're sending a message. The Valentis think they can outmaneuver us, but we'll show them that they're playing in our world, by our rules."

The men nodded, their expressions a mix of anticipation and respect. They knew the stakes, and they knew I wasn't one to make empty threats.

We spent the next hour finalizing the plan, going over every detail until there were no gaps, no room for error. Every operation hinged on precision—on our ability to outthink and outplay our enemies without firing a single shot. The Valenti family had been restless ever since I stepped into my father's shoes, testing boundaries, probing for weaknesses. They saw my transition into leadership as an opportunity—not just to challenge the Navarras but to establish themselves as a force in New York's underworld.

The Valentis weren't just another rival family; they were dangerous because they were unpredictable. Their patriarch, Vito Valenti, was known for his erratic temper and reckless ambition. He had built his reputation through brute force, but his methods often left trails of chaos behind. For years, the Navarras had kept them in check, using calculated diplomacy where violence wasn't necessary. But since my father's absence due to health issues, that balance had begun to tip. The Valentis thought the Navarra empire was fragile without him at the helm. Tonight, I intended to prove them wrong.

As the meeting adjourned, I lingered behind, letting the others filter out of the room. Nico stayed back, his sharp eyes watching me with a knowing look.

"You've got something on your mind," he said, his tone casual but with an edge of concern. "Care to share?"

I sighed, running a hand through my hair. "It's just...this is more than a power play. If we win tonight, it'll force the Valentis into a corner. They're dangerous when they're desperate."

Nico nodded, his expression thoughtful. "Desperation makes people unpredictable. But it also makes them sloppy. If they come at us, they'll do it without thinking. And that's when we strike."

I looked at him, appreciating his confidence, but knowing that the road ahead was treacherous. "We'll have to watch our backs. They won't go down quietly."

"Neither will we," Nico replied, a hint of a smile on his lips. "The Valentis might think they know how to play this game, but they've forgotten one thing—you've been watching and learning from the best. You've got your father's fire, but your grandfather's cunning. That's what makes you dangerous."

His words were meant to reassure, but they only reminded me of the burden I carried. I had to live up to the Navarra name, to the expectations of those who followed me, while also protecting what little self-awareness I had left. And tonight would be a test of everything I'd learned.

Just as Nico turned to leave, I caught movement from the corner of my eye—Marco was waiting, leaning casually against the doorframe, his arms crossed. The others had already gone, leaving the room eerily quiet except for the faint hum of the air conditioner.

I exhaled and gestured toward the doorway. "Come on, Marco. Say what you're thinking."

He pushed off the frame and sauntered toward me, his footsteps measured, deliberate. "It's not what I'm thinking that matters, Alessandra. It's what everyone else is starting to think."

I narrowed my eyes. "And what's that?"

"That your father's absence has gone on long enough." His voice was soft, but the implication hit like a punch to the gut. "They respect you, sure. But they respected him in a way that kept rivals like the Valentis from pulling stunts like this in the first place."

I crossed my arms, not backing down. "My father is recovering. That's all they need to know."

Marco's gaze hardened, the weight of his concern bearing down on me. "You know it won't stay quiet forever. People talk. They speculate. Right now, you've got control—but if the wrong people start to sense weakness, the Valentis won't be the only problem knocking at our door."

I clenched my jaw, swallowing the knot of frustration building in my throat. He wasn't wrong, but that didn't mean I was ready to concede to his pessimism. "We're not weak," I said sharply. "Tonight will prove that."

Marco studied me, his expression unreadable. "I'm not questioning your ability to handle tonight's operation. But what happens after that? How long do you think you can hold them off before they demand answers?"

I stepped closer, lowering my voice. "Long enough. My father will recover. Until then, I don't need them to love me. I need them to fear what happens if they don't follow me."

He was quiet for a moment, then nodded, accepting my answer—for now. "Just remember, fear only lasts as long as the results do. Keep winning, and they'll stay in line. But the second they see you slip..." He didn't need to finish the sentence. The warning was clear.

"I won't slip," I said, my voice cold, resolute. "Let them think what they want. As long as I'm running this family, they'll fall in line."

Marco sighed, running a hand through his salt-and-pepper hair. "Then make sure tonight's flawless, Alessandra. Because if it's not, the Valentis won't just be a nuisance—they'll become a threat we can't ignore."

I watched him leave, the weight of his words hanging over me. He was right, of course. I hated that he was right. But that didn't mean I was going to let him see the cracks forming beneath the surface. I had spent a year proving that I belonged in this world, and tonight would be no different.

As I made my way to the car, Nico waiting by the driver's seat, I took a steadying breath. The Valentis were desperate, reckless, and arrogant enough to think they could push us out. But tonight, I would remind them—and everyone else—why the Navarras had survived for generations.

Because we didn't just play the game.

We owned it.

By the time we reached the Valenti's chosen meeting spot—a dimly lit dockside warehouse—the night was well underway. The docks were quiet, the only sounds the gentle lapping of the waves against the piers and the distant hum of the city. The air was thick with the smell of saltwater and oil, a perfect backdrop for a deal that would never make it into any official books. It was the kind of place where alliances were formed or broken, and lives were sometimes the cost of either. They were also considered neutral territory.

The Valentis had chosen this spot carefully, probably thinking they were out of reach. The docks were just remote enough to avoid prying eyes but close enough to the city for a quick exit if things turned south. But they had miscalculated. These docks were as much ours as they were anyone else's, and tonight, I planned to remind them of that.

As I stood outside the warehouse, the cold night air biting at my skin, I knew this was more than just an operation—it was a message, one that needed to echo through the underworld. The Valentis had been restless ever since I stepped into leadership, probing for weaknesses, pushing boundaries. They saw my father's absence as an opening, a sign that the Navarras were vulnerable. But tonight, I would shatter that illusion.

The briefcase of money inside wasn't just cash—it was a symbol of ambition, a down payment on a future the Valentis thought they could secure by allying with the Giordanos. But power wasn't something you bought with bills. It was something you took and held on to through fear, loyalty, and strategy. The Valentis didn't understand that yet, but they would soon.

We arrived early, blending into the shadows as we took

up our positions. My heart pounded steadily, adrenaline heightening my senses. The scent of the sea filled my lungs, grounding me as I prepared for what came next. I watched the entrance, waiting for the right moment to strike.

Nico sidled up next to me, his footsteps silent on the gravel. His sharp eyes flicked to mine, reading me as easily as ever. "You know what this deal means to them, don't you?" he murmured, his voice low.

I nodded. "They think a briefcase of cash and a few crates of guns will earn them the loyalty of the Giordanos." My voice was steady, but inside, I could feel the storm brewing. "But they don't understand that money alone isn't enough. The Giordanos value strength and control. If we take that briefcase, we're not just taking their money—we're weakening their credibility."

Nico chuckled darkly, shaking his head. "Without credibility, they've got nothing. The Giordanos won't ally with a family that can't even protect their own deals. They'll see the Valentis as weak, and they'll walk away without looking back."

"Exactly," I replied, my resolve hardening.

At exactly midnight, the Valentis and the Giordanos arrived, their sleek black cars gliding to a stop at the edge of the warehouse. I watched as they got out, their movements confident, almost cocky. They thought this was their night, their moment to solidify an alliance that would tip the scales in their favor.

But they were wrong.

I signaled to Nico, who nodded and slipped away, moving like a shadow through the darkness.

Minutes passed like hours as the two families exchanged pleasantries. The Valentis were putting on a show of strength, but I could see the cracks. Vito Valenti—

the family patriarch—stood at the center, his gaze hard but his posture tense. He was a man driven by ambition but plagued by impatience, a dangerous combination that often led to reckless decisions.

Several Valenti guards stood nearby, their hands hovering near their weapons. The Giordanos had brought muscle too—men in tailored suits with guns holstered discreetly under their jackets. But they weren't the only ones armed. My men were stationed along the perimeter, hidden in the shadows, their fingers resting lightly on their triggers. If things went south, the Navarras were ready to handle it.

Finally, Vito opened the briefcase, revealing neat stacks of crisp bills. The Giordano representative reached for it, his fingers grazing the edges of the cash. And that was when we made our move.

Nico stepped out of the shadows along with several of our men, a smirk playing on his lips as he casually lit a cigarette. "Evening, gentlemen," he drawled, the flicker of the lighter illuminating his face just enough for them to recognize him. "I see you're conducting some business. Mind if I cut in?"

The Valentis froze, their eyes narrowing as they realized they'd been set up. Several of their guards shifted uneasily, but the Navarra men blocked any chance of retreat, guns raised in silent warning. Vito's hand inched toward his gun, but he hesitated. That was his first mistake.

"You've got a lot of nerve showing up here," Vito hissed.

"I've got more than that," Nico replied, blowing out a cloud of smoke. "I've got an offer. One you might want to hear before you do something you'll regret."

Louis Giordano, a shrewd man with silver hair and sharp eyes, hesitated. He glanced at Vito, then back at Nico, weighing his options. And that hesitation was all we needed.

I stepped forward with six more of our men, their guns casually slung, some taken directly from the Valenti shipment. "The money stays with us," I said, my tone leaving no room for argument. "And in return, you walk away."

Vito's eyes jumped to me, recognition dawning as he realized who he was dealing with. "Alessandra Navarra," he said slowly, his voice dripping with disdain. "So the rumors are true. The Navarra princess is playing at being queen."

I didn't flinch. Instead, I smiled—a cold, calculated expression. "I'm here to correct a mistake. The Valentis think they can buy their way into power with a briefcase of cash, but power isn't for sale. It's taken. And tonight, we're taking it."

Nico casually stepped forward, his hand resting on the briefcase.

Louis raised an eyebrow, clearly intrigued. "This is an unexpected development."

I turned my gaze to him, my voice calm but firm. "The Navarras don't make deals in the shadows. We control the shadows. And you know as well as I do that an alliance with us is worth more than anything the Valentis could offer. They're trying to buy your loyalty. We're offering you something far more valuable—stability."

Nico opened the briefcase, revealing the stacks of cash inside. He smirked at Vito, who was visibly sweating now.

"Your money's still here," Nico said, his voice dripping with contempt. "But your leverage? That's gone. Walk away while you still can."

Vito opened his mouth to argue, but I silenced him with a look, my eyes cold and unforgiving.

"This isn't a negotiation. It's a warning," I said, each

word heavy with intent. "You've overstepped, and now you're paying the price. If you want to survive in this city, you'll remember who's really in charge."

The Valentis, realizing they had been outmaneuvered, slowly backed down. Mr. Giordano smiled thinly.

"It seems the balance of power is clear," he said, inclining his head slightly. "We'll be in touch, Miss Navarra."

As I watched the Valentis slink away, their pride bruised and their ambitions shattered, I knew the repercussions of tonight's actions would ripple through the underworld. But for now, we had secured our place at the top. And I had proven that strength wasn't about who was in charge. It was about who came out on top when the bottom fell out.

Chapter 32

Burying the Past

Steven

The sound of gunfire echoed through the narrow streets, reverberating off the crumbling walls of the war-torn city. I ducked behind a rusted car, my heart pounding in my chest as I tried to steady my breathing. The air was thick with dust and smoke, the acrid smell of burning rubber and gasoline stinging my eyes.

I had been embedded with these rebel forces for nearly two years, documenting their fight against a corrupt regime that had turned their homeland into a battlefield. It was dangerous, dirty work—the kind that most people would avoid at all costs. But it was the kind of work I lived for. The kind of work that made me feel alive, that made the rest of the world fade away.

I peeked over the edge of the car, my camera clutched tightly in my hands. Through the viewfinder, I could see the rebel fighters advancing, their faces grim and determined. The city was a maze of ruins, a place where every corner could hide a sniper, every shadow a trap. But they moved forward with a purpose, driven by the need to take back what had been stolen from them.

A rocket exploded nearby, sending debris flying through the air. I didn't flinch. My focus was entirely on the shot, on capturing the raw, unfiltered reality of the war. I had seen it all—death, destruction, the loss of innocence—but it never got any easier. It just became... routine.

My work had taken me to some of the darkest corners of the world, places where hope was a distant memory and survival was a daily struggle. And I had documented it all, telling the stories that needed to be told, exposing the truths that those in power wanted to keep hidden. It was dangerous, yes. But it was also necessary.

The rebels reached the edge of the city square, their advance slowed by the heavy resistance from government forces. I moved closer, careful to stay in the shadows, to avoid drawing attention. My heart raced as I raised my camera, capturing the tension, the fear, the bravery etched into the faces of those fighting for their freedom.

This was what I lived for—the adrenaline, the risk, the knowledge that what I was doing mattered. But as the firefight continued, as bullets whizzed past my head and the ground shook with the force of explosions, I felt something else creeping in. Something I hadn't allowed myself to feel in a long time.

Fatigue.

Not just the physical exhaustion that came from being in a war zone for so long, but the emotional toll of living on the edge, of constantly running from my past. I had buried myself in this work, using it as a shield, a way to keep myself from thinking too much about everything I had lost. Even after five years, I couldn't break free.

Now, standing in the middle of this hell, I couldn't

escape the truth anymore. I was tired. Tired of the violence, the fear, the never-ending cycle of death and destruction. Tired of running from a life that I couldn't forget, no matter how hard I tried.

The feel of my satellite phone vibrating in my pocket jolted me back to the present. I ducked behind a wall, away from the chaos, and answered it, the noise of the battle fading into the background.

"Porter," I said, my voice rough from the dust and smoke.

"Steven, it's Andrew," came the voice on the other end, my editor from the news agency. "We need you to come home."

The words hit me like a punch to the gut. Home. I had been home three times in the last five years. If I was getting a call to come home, it couldn't be good.

"What's going on?" I asked, forcing my voice to stay steady.

There was a pause, a hesitation that told me everything I needed to know. "It's your father. He's fading fast. You need to get back to New York."

For a moment, the world seemed to stop. The sounds of the battle, the fear, the adrenaline—all of it faded away, leaving only the stark, undeniable truth. My father was dying, and I was half a world away, surrounded by a war that wasn't mine to fight.

"I'll be on the next flight out," I said, my voice tight with emotion.

"I'm sorry, Steven," Andrew said softly. "Take care of yourself."

The call ended, and I stood there, the phone still in my hand, the weight of the news pressing down on me.

The flight back to New York was long. I spent the hours lost in a haze of exhaustion and grief. By the time I landed, I knew it was too late. My father was gone.

The funeral was small, just close family and friends, the kind of gathering that my father would have preferred. My brothers and I stood together, trying to hold each other up as best we could. My mother's grief was palpable, a heavy, suffocating presence that seemed to fill the room. We were all struggling, all trying to make sense of a world without him.

That night, after everyone had left, I found myself sitting in the living room with Nate, nursing a glass of whiskey. The house was too quiet, the absence of my father like a hole in the fabric of our lives.

"You staying?" Nate asked, his voice low.

I stared at the amber liquid swirling in my glass, unsure how to answer. "I don't know. I was only supposed to be here for the funeral."

"You think you should just jump back into a war zone after this?" His voice wasn't harsh, but it carried the authority of someone who'd spent years interrogating suspects and reading between the lines.

I bristled at the comment, but there was no malice in it —just honesty. And maybe that's what hurt the most, knowing that he was right.

"Mom misses you, Steven. Mitch too. He's putting on a brave face, but you know how he is. The two of you were always close."

Until we weren't. Until I left and hardly looked back. I could hear the subtext loud and clear.

I exhaled sharply, the weight of expectation pressing

down on me. "I've been working," I said, the words feeling hollow.

"I know," Nate replied, leaning back in the chair. "But this isn't work, Steven. This is family. You've got a choice—don't let the next funeral be the only other time we see you."

The next morning, my mother pulled me aside while I was pouring coffee. Her eyes were red from crying, but there was a quiet strength in her voice. "Stay, Steven. Just for a while. Let yourself breathe."

Let yourself breathe. I didn't even know what that would feel like anymore. But it sounded like a good idea.

Days after the funeral, I drove down and wandered the City, letting the familiar sights and sounds wash over me. New York had always felt like home, but now it felt foreign, like a place I no longer belonged. Everywhere I looked, I saw reminders of the life I had lost—the life that had disappeared just as suddenly as my father.

I hadn't thought of her in a long time, but now, being back in the city where we had once dreamed of a future together, it all came rushing back. The pain, the confusion, the love that had never truly died.

But could I stay?

If I did, I needed something to anchor me, something to keep me from getting lost in the grief and the memories. I wasn't sure I was ready to stop moving. The thought of staying still terrified me more than bullets or jungle guerrillas ever had.

I also discovered that The City apparently had a way of digging up old wounds, of reminding you of the things you had lost. I'd been across the street from a café we'd frequented on the weekends just before we ventured into our favorite bookstore. That's when I saw her. Or at least, I thought I had.

The woman was standing on the other side of the street, her back to me, her long dark hair flowing down her back. My heart stopped, the breath catching in my throat when she turned her head in my direction. It immediately sent my heart and mind racing.

It couldn't be. It wasn't possible. But something deep inside me screamed that it was her.

Before I could cross the street, she turned, disappearing into the crowd, swallowed up by the city that more hers than mine now. I stood there, frozen, the moment slipping away as quickly as it had come.

It had to have been her. Or was my mind just playing tricks on me, teasing me with ghosts that refused to stay buried?

I didn't know. But as I stood there, staring at the spot where she had been, I felt something stir inside me—something I had thought I had buried.

Curiosity? Obsession? Love? Whatever it was, it was as strong as ever and was now rushing back in at full force.

Being back in New York wasn't supposed to be part of the plan. I was only back for the funeral, just passing through. Now, I wasn't so sure. Because if Alessandra was here, if she had never left... Everything was about to change. I could feel it.

Chapter 33

Reminders

Alessandra

I didn't need to read the obituary twice to feel the impact. It was as if the words on the page reached out and struck me in the chest, a sharp reminder of so many things I had lost. Steven's father had passed away, and with him, another piece of the life I had left behind crumbled into dust.

I sat in the darkened room, the light of my computer screen casting shadows on the walls, making the space feel even more suffocating. The obituary was simple, just a few lines about his life and the family he left behind. But it was enough to send a wave of grief crashing over me. He had been so kind to me, welcoming me into his home, his family, without hesitation. And now, he was gone.

My hand trembled as I reached for the glass of water on the table beside me. I hadn't planned to react like this, hadn't allowed myself to think of Steven or his family in a long time. But seeing the obituary, reading those words, it all came rushing back—the warmth of his father's smile, the way he treated me like a daughter from the moment we met, the dinners, the laughter, the feeling of being part of something good and pure, something I knew I could never have again.

I had told myself I wouldn't go. It was too dangerous, too risky. But the more I tried to push the thought away, the more it clung to me, demanding my attention. I knew I had no right to be there, no right to mourn a man who wasn't truly mine to grieve. But how could I stay away?

The funeral was small, intimate—just close family and friends. I stood at a distance, hidden behind a cluster of trees that bordered the cemetery, my heart heavy with the weight of what I was doing. I could see them all—Steven, his brothers, their mother—each of them locked in their own grief, their faces drawn and pale. I felt like an intruder, a ghost haunting a place where I no longer belonged.

My breath caught in my throat when I saw Steven, his face etched with sorrow, his eyes hollow and lost. I hadn't seen him in years, hadn't allowed myself to imagine what he might look like now. But here he was, so close yet so far from the life we had once shared. He looked different, older, harder, as if the time apart had taken its toll on him too. But in the shadows of his grief, I could still see the man I had loved, the man I still loved, no matter how hard I tried to bury those feelings.

I had planned to leave as soon as the service was over, to slip away unnoticed before anyone could see me. But I couldn't bring myself to move. Not yet. I needed to see him, to feel close to him, even if only for a moment.

As the mourners began to disperse, I took a step forward, moving closer to the edge of the cemetery. The wind picked up, rustling the leaves in the trees, carrying with it the faint sound of their voices. I watched as Steven placed a hand on his mother's shoulder, offering her a small, comforting smile. My heart ached at the sight, the pain of knowing I would never be part of that world again was nearly unbearable.

Before anyone could notice me, I turned away, slipping through the trees and back onto the quiet path that led out of the cemetery. But as I moved further from the crowd, a memory stopped me in my tracks—the last time I saw his father.

It was a summer evening, the kind that hummed with warmth and possibility. Steven and I had been at his family's house for dinner. His father had laughed at one of my stories, the sound rich and booming, filling the room like sunshine. As we said goodbye, he had squeezed my hand and said, *Take care of my son. He's a good one, you know.*

I had smiled, promising him that I would.

The weight of that broken promise settled over me like a shroud. I squeezed my eyes shut, willing the memory away. But no amount of distance could erase it.

I kept walking.

Several days after the funeral I had business in the City. I'd told Nico I needed to walk and clear my mind after the meeting I'd just left but the truth was I'd been unable to shake the dark cloud that had lingered after seeing Steven and his family from afar.

Ducking into a small café, I ordered a coffee, but the cup sat untouched on the table in front of me as I tried to steady my nerves. The past, the memories, the emotions—they all swirled together in a storm that I couldn't calm. I knew I should call Nico and head back home, but my legs felt heavy, as if weighed down by the past I was still running from but didn't really want to escape.

I was certain that if I ever fully let go, I'd lose myself completely and have no chance of redemption. At least by holding on to the tiny sliver of who I might have been all those years ago, I could believe that there was still something worth saving. That sliver kept me grounded.

Finally, I forced myself to stand, leaving the café with a quick glance around to ensure I wasn't being watched. The late afternoon sun cast long shadows across the sidewalk as I stepped out into the bustling street, blending into the flow of pedestrians.

I felt it before I saw him—the heavy weight of someone's gaze boring into me, like a warning sent straight to my gut. My breath hitched as I looked up.

Steven.

He was standing on the other side of the street, his gaze locked on mine. The recognition hit him like lightning, sparking something raw and vulnerable in his eyes. For a moment, I was frozen. My heart pounded, the sounds of the city fading into a distant hum.

Move, Alessandra.

I turned sharply, blending into the sea of people, my pulse racing as I navigated the crowded streets. The noise of the city surged back in—a blaring taxi horn, the chatter of passersby—but all I could hear was the rapid thudding of my heartbeat.

I didn't dare look back.

My heart raced as I hurried down the sidewalk, the sound of my footsteps echoing in my ears, mingling with the hum of the city.

I missed him. I missed the life we had, the dreams we

shared. But that life was over, and I had no place in it anymore. That didn't stop the longing.

The city streets blurred as I walked, my mind racing, my emotions in turmoil. I shouldn't have come. I knew that now. Seeing Steven again, seeing the pain in his eyes, had only reopened wounds that had never been allowed to fully heal. I had tried so hard to forget, to move on, to bury the part of me that still longed for him. But being here, in this city, so close to him, had shattered all those defenses.

I slowed as I neared the park, the same one we used to walk through, hand in hand, dreaming of a future that would never be. The memories flooded back, each one more painful than the last, each one a reminder of what I had sacrificed.

Steven had been my light, the one bright spot in a world that had been filled with darkness for so long. But that light had been snuffed out, and all that was left was the shadow of who I used to be. The woman he loved was gone, replaced by someone colder, harder, someone who had learned to survive in a world that demanded nothing less.

I reached the park and found a bench tucked away from the main path, a place where I could sit and catch my breath. The city moved on around me, oblivious to the storm raging inside me. I had been so careful, so determined to stay hidden, to keep my distance. But all it had taken was one look, one moment of weakness, and now everything felt like it was unraveling.

I leaned forward, resting my elbows on my knees, my head in my hands. The tears I had held back for so long finally began to fall, each one a release of the pain I had buried deep within me. I didn't make a sound, didn't want to draw any attention to myself. This was my burden to bear, my punishment for daring to love someone I could never truly have.

I didn't know how long I sat there, lost in my grief, the city continuing to move around me as if nothing had changed. Eventually, I knew I had to get up, to keep moving, to disappear back into the shadows where I belonged. I couldn't let Steven find me, couldn't let him get pulled back into the life I had tried so hard to protect him from.

I stood, wiping the tears from my face, forcing myself to breathe, to push the pain down where it couldn't reach me. I had to let go of that moment in the cemetery, had to convince myself that it had been nothing more than a fleeting glance, a trick of the light.

He hadn't really seen me. He couldn't have.

Deep down, I knew the truth. He had seen me. And Steven Porter wasn't the kind of man to let ghosts fade quietly into the night. Not without a fight.

He would come looking. And when he did, I wasn't sure I'd have the strength to walk away again.

Chapter 34

Moving Forward

Steven

The quiet settled in the house like a thick blanket, heavy and oppressive. It was a different kind of silence, the kind that came after loss—a silence that filled every corner, reminding you of what was missing. My mother and I had been living in this silence since the funeral, each of us navigating the grief in our own way, but always coming back to each other for comfort.

Dad's absence was felt in every room. The house was the same, yet completely different without him. His favorite chair by the fireplace, the spot at the kitchen table where he always read the morning paper, the tools in the garage he would tinker with on weekends—they were all there, untouched, but the man who gave them life was gone.

I found myself lingering in those spaces, half-expecting to hear his voice or see him walk in with that familiar, reassuring smile. But all that greeted me was the echo of memories, a bittersweet reminder of the moments we had shared.

As I walked past the garage, the familiar scent of motor

oil hit me, and before I knew it, I was standing in front of my father's old workbench. The tools were neatly arranged —just like he'd left them. I remembered being a kid, sitting on a stool while he fixed the car, listening to him talk about responsibility, about how sometimes life isn't about what you want—it's about what you need to do.

"You'll figure it out," he'd said once when I told him I didn't know what I wanted to do after college. "Just don't be afraid to change direction when you need to."

My mother had taken to the garden in the mornings, her way of keeping busy, of finding a small semblance of peace amidst the chaos of grief. I would watch her from the kitchen window, her hands moving methodically through the soil, tending to the flowers with a care that spoke of decades of routine and love. It hurt to see her alone out there, tending to a garden she had once shared with my father. But it was what she needed, and I respected that.

We had stayed in touch even when I was across the ocean or deep in a jungle, but since Dad's death, it was like we were holding each other up, each of us leaning on the other to keep from falling apart. In the evenings, we would sit together in the living room, sharing stories about Dad, sometimes laughing, sometimes crying. There was something healing about it, about remembering the good times, about acknowledging the loss together.

One evening, after dinner, we sat at the kitchen table, the dishes still piled in the sink, the last of the sunlight filtering through the window. The silence between us wasn't uncomfortable; it was the kind of silence that came from understanding, from knowing that words weren't always necessary.

"I'm glad you're here," Mom said suddenly, her voice

soft and warm. "I don't know what I would've done without you these past few weeks."

"I'm glad I'm here too," I replied, reaching across the table to squeeze her hand.

She smiled, but there was a sadness in her eyes that hadn't been there before. "I just wish your father could've seen how far you've come. He was so proud of you, Steven. We both were."

I swallowed the lump in my throat, nodding. "I know. And I'm grateful for that."

She paused, her gaze drifting to the window, the garden just visible in the fading light. "What are you going to do now?" she asked, her tone gentle, as if she was afraid of the answer.

"I'm not sure," I admitted. "I've been thinking about taking some time off, maybe staying here for a while longer. It's been years since I had any real time off, and... well, I think I need it."

She nodded, her expression thoughtful. "That sounds like a good idea. You've been running nonstop for so long, Steven. Maybe it's time to slow down, to figure out if you're running to or from something."

"I think you're right," I said, sighing. "It's just... it's hard to think about slowing down. I love my work, but after everything that's happened, I'm not sure if it's enough anymore."

Mom reached out, covering my hand with hers. "Take the time you need, honey. You've done so much already, and there's no rush to figure it all out. Your father would want you to be happy, to find something that fulfills you."

I nodded, her words sinking in. "I'll let my editor know I'm taking some time off. I think I need it, more than I realized."

Later that night, after I sent off the email to my editor, I sat in the quiet of my childhood bedroom, the familiar surroundings both comforting and strange. The room had barely changed since I left for college, the posters on the walls, the bookshelves lined with novels and magazines, the desk cluttered with old notebooks and pens. It was a time capsule of a different life, one that felt distant and almost surreal now.

I leaned back in the old desk chair, running a hand through my hair as I thought about the conversation with my mother. She was right—I needed to slow down, to take stock of what I really wanted. The last few years had been a whirlwind of assignments, one dangerous story after another, each one pulling me further away from the life I had once imagined for myself.

I had spent so long running from my past, from the pain of losing Alessandra, that I hadn't allowed myself to really process any of it. And now, with my father's death, it was all coming back, forcing me to confront the emotions I had buried deep inside.

I thought back to a few days ago, the moment when I saw her. Or at least, I thought I had. Just a glimpse of her dark hair catching the light in a way that was unmistakably Alessandra. My heart had slammed into my ribs, and for a second, the world tilted. But by the time I crossed the street to get a better look, the woman was gone.

I had stood there for several minutes, scanning the sidewalk, telling myself it couldn't have been her. My mind had to be playing tricks on me, dredging up ghosts when I was already emotionally raw. She wasn't in New York. She couldn't be. I had spent months searching for her after she left, and if she'd wanted me to find her, I would have by now.

Still, the doubt gnawed at me, leaving a dull ache in my chest that wouldn't go away.

A few days later, I was leaving a restaurant where I'd met Mitch for lunch when I heard someone call my name. I turned to see a familiar face—Sam, an old acquaintance from college I hadn't seen in years. He was sitting at one of the outdoor tables, a newspaper in hand, his expression one of pleasant surprise.

"Steven Porter? Is that you?" he asked, standing up to greet me.

"Sam," I replied, a smile tugging at my lips despite the heaviness in my chest. "It's been a long time."

"Too long," he agreed, clapping me on the shoulder. "What are you doing here? I thought you were off chasing stories around the world."

"I was," I said, shrugging. "But I'm back for now. My dad... he passed away a few weeks ago."

Sam's expression softened, his hand dropping to his side. "I'm sorry to hear that. I'm sure that's been hard."

"Thanks," I said, nodding. "Yeah, it's been rough, but we're getting through it."

"Of course," he said, gesturing to the chair across from him. "Are you free to sit for a bit? Catch up?"

I hesitated for a moment, then nodded. "Yeah, I'd like that."

We found a café with an outdoor seating space where we spent the next hour talking, reminiscing about our college days, the paths our lives had taken since then. It was good to talk to someone who knew me before everything got so complicated, someone who understood where I had come from.

As the conversation shifted to more recent events, Sam mentioned that he was working for a news site in the city, a place that had been making waves in investigative journalism. "We've actually got an opening, if you're interested," he said, glancing at me over the rim of his coffee cup. "I know you've been doing some amazing work abroad, but if you ever feel like staying put for a while, we could use someone with your experience."

I considered his offer, the idea of staying in New York suddenly not as unappealing as it had been before. "I might be in touch," I said, not committing to anything just yet but leaving the door open.

"Take your time," Sam said, smiling. "The city could use someone like you. And it'd be good to get to know you again."

I thanked him and a few minutes later we left the café. The thought of settling in New York gnawed at me. I wanted to believe I could handle being here—that I could stay still without feeling like I was suffocating. But the truth was, I wasn't sure. The adrenaline, the thrill of running headfirst into chaos, had become my coping mechanism. Could I really give that up? Could I even sit at a desk, knowing the world was still burning out there?

Walking through the neighboring park, the distant sound of a saxophone echoed off the walls of a nearby building. The melody reminded me of late-night walks with Alessandra, the way we'd get lost in the city without a plan, just chasing moments. I closed my eyes, letting the memory wash over me like a wave I couldn't control. She was everywhere here, in the cracks of the sidewalk, in the hum of the city's pulse.

I imagined what life might be like if I took Sam's offer. The idea of a steady routine, of waking up in the same bed every morning without the thrill of danger waiting on the other side of the world, felt foreign. Could I do it? Could I stay grounded in a city that held both everything and nothing for me?

For the first time since coming home, I felt like maybe, just maybe, I could start to move forward. I didn't know what the future held, but I was beginning to think that it might not be as bleak as I had feared.

But even as I tried to focus on the future, the past still lingered, just out of reach, refusing to let me go. I had come back to New York to say goodbye to one part of my life. But something told me I wasn't leaving without confronting another.

Chapter 35

A Fresh Start

Steven

The days following my conversation with Sam were filled with contemplation and new resolve. The idea of staying in New York had started as a faint whisper, but it quickly grew into something more—a need, a calling I couldn't ignore. I spent hours walking the city, revisiting old haunts and exploring new ones, trying to reconcile the past with the present. The pull of this place was stronger than I'd expected, and the more I thought about it, the more I realized I wasn't ready to leave. Not yet.

It was late one evening, after another long day of wandering the city, when I found myself sitting on the edge of my bed in the room I had slept in as a child. My mother's house was quiet, the comforting silence of familiarity wrapping around me like a blanket. But instead of comfort, I felt the stirrings of restlessness—a need to move forward, to find something to anchor me in the here and now.

The next morning, I made the decision. Over breakfast,

I told my mother I was going to take the job Sam had mentioned.

She looked at me with a mixture of surprise and relief, her hand pausing over the teacup she was about to lift to her lips. "That's wonderful, Steven," she said, her voice warm. "I think it's the right move. It'll give you something to focus on, something to ground you."

I nodded, feeling the weight of the decision settle in my chest, not heavy, but solid. "I think so too. I've been running for a long time, Mom. Maybe it's time to stop and... figure things out."

She smiled, a soft, knowing smile that only mothers have. "You're not running anymore, honey. You're choosing to stay. And that's a big difference."

Her words echoed in my mind as I made the call to Sam, accepting the position at the news site. The process moved quickly—faster than I had anticipated. Within days, I found myself back in the rhythm of work, the familiar buzz of the newsroom invigorating in a way I hadn't felt in a long time.

I decided it would be better to find my own place, both for my sake and for my mother's. We had shared the initial wave of grief, but now it was time for both of us to begin healing, to find our new normal. The apartment I rented wasn't far from the office, a small but comfortable place where I could be alone with my thoughts when I needed to be and immerse myself in work when the silence became too much.

Sam welcomed me to the team with the easy camaraderie of old acquaintances, and before long, I was knee-deep in my first big assignment. It started as an investigation into a small case of corruption at the local government level—just a series of whispers about bribery and misuse of funds. The kind of story that could either be a quick win or lead down a rabbit hole, depending on what we uncovered.

I started with the basics, interviewing sources, combing through public records, piecing together the fragments of information that didn't quite add up. It wasn't long before the trail led me to something bigger, something that sent a familiar thrill through my veins. There were connections—small, barely visible at first—but they were there, linking the local corruption to a crime syndicate operating in the shadows of the city.

As I dug deeper, the connections became clearer, the pieces of the puzzle falling into place. The name Navarra came up more than once, in hushed tones and off-the-record comments. It was a name I hadn't heard said aloud in years, but it was one I could never forget.

The first time I saw the name Navarra in the files, my breath hitched. My fingers hovered over the page, reluctant to move forward, as if saying the name aloud would breathe life into old wounds. Memories of Alessandra flooded back —her smile, her voice, the way she left without a word.

I pushed those thoughts aside and forced myself to focus. It wasn't long before I realized that the syndicate linked directly to the government corruption was the Navarra family—the most powerful and feared crime family in New York. The very same family that had ripped Alessandra from my life and sent me spiraling into the chaos of the past few years.

I knew that pursuing this story could lead me down a path I might not be ready to take. But the journalist in me—the part of me that had always been driven by the need to uncover the truth, no matter the cost—couldn't resist. The stakes were high, but so were the potential rewards. And if this story could bring some of the most dangerous people in the city to justice, how could I walk away?

One of my recent sources, a city council staffer, had been skittish from the start. But during our last meeting, she was practically shaking. "I've said too much already," she whispered, glancing over her shoulder. "Just be careful, Steven. These people don't play fair."

The deeper I went, the more I found myself on edge. There was something about this investigation that felt personal, something that made the hairs on the back of my neck stand on end. I was getting close to something—something big, something that had been hidden for a long time. And I had the sinking feeling that whatever it was, it was connected to Alessandra Navarra whose last name appeared in my research too many times to be a fluke.

I sat back in my chair, staring at the notes scattered across my desk, the names, dates, and connections swirling in my mind. The thrill of the chase, the excitement of being on the brink of a major story—it was all there. But so was something else, something darker, something I couldn't quite put my finger on.

I took a deep breath, trying to steady my nerves. I was getting close. And the closer I got, the more I realized that this wasn't just another story. This was becoming personal. It was about more than just exposing corruption. This was about finding the truth, no matter where it led, no matter what it cost.

And all I could think was that the cost was going to be higher than I could have ever imagined.

Chapter 36

Going in Blind

Alessandra

The city had always been a refuge—a place where I could lose myself in the noise and the crowds, where I could be anonymous. But now, as I sat in the back of a sleek black car, winding through the streets of Manhattan, that anonymity felt like a prison. The world outside was vibrant and alive, a stark contrast to the turmoil churning inside me.

Aside from the brief glimpse at the funeral, it had been years since I'd last been close to him. I had forced myself to stop looking at his social media pages and keeping tabs on his family after about a year once he left New York. I convinced myself to sever the last ties to the life I had once dreamed of and had thrown myself into my role within the Navarra family, burying my emotions beneath layers of duty and ruthlessness. But even as I built a new identity, the past refused to stay buried. And now, it was all crashing back onto me, more forcefully than I could have ever anticipated.

I stared out the tinted window, the cityscape blurring as the car sped through the streets. My phone buzzed in my lap, a message from one of our operatives confirming what I had feared: Steven was back in New York for good, and he was getting too close.

It wasn't just a simple investigation anymore. He was digging into the Navarra family, where there were secrets that had been kept hidden for generations. Secrets that could destroy him and many others if he uncovered the wrong ones.

My chest tightened as I read the report, detailing his every move, his relentless pursuit of the truth. I could see it all unfolding in my mind—Steven, driven by his need to uncover the facts, following a trail that would inevitably lead him straight to my family. Straight to me. And while I would welcome him with open arms, my father would not.

The thought of him in danger, of him unknowingly walking into the dragon's lair, made my blood run cold. Steven was brilliant, resourceful, and tenacious—qualities that had made me fall in love with him. But those same qualities could now be his undoing. The Navarra family didn't forgive, and they certainly didn't forget. If Steven kept pushing, kept digging, he would find himself caught in a web that was impossible to escape.

My hands clenched into fists, the pressure of my nails digging into my palms grounding me as I fought to stay calm. I had worked so hard to keep him safe, to keep him away from this world. But now, it seemed my efforts had been in vain.

And I was pretty sure any request I made of him to stop his digging would be met with a less than warm reception, but I had to try.

"Miss Navarra?" My driver's voice cut through my

thoughts, bringing me back to the present. "We're approaching the building."

I took a deep breath, forcing myself to focus. "Good," I replied, my voice steady despite the storm raging inside me. "Park around the corner. I'll go in alone."

The driver nodded, and a few minutes later, the car eased to a stop. I glanced at the location on my phone one last time. The building in front of me was nondescript, blending into the surrounding cityscape. But I wasn't here for the aesthetics. This building housed a certain newsroom where I knew a certain award-winning journalist worked and he was exactly who I needed to see.

As I walked around the side of the building and through the front door, my mind raced with the decision that lay before me. I knew I couldn't let Steven continue down this path. But the thought of confronting him, of stepping back into his life after everything that had happened, filled me with dread.

I kept my head lowered as I moved through the hallways with purpose. According the one of our guys, Steven's office was on the second floor so I took the stairs while trying to control my breathing and slow my racing heart. I was by no means out of shape. I just hadn't felt this level of anxiety in a very long time.

His door was closed, the nameplate clearly naming it his. I stood in front of the door for several moments, my hand hovering over the handle as I hesitated. Once I crossed this threshold, there would be no turning back. I would be wordlessly admitting things that had only been assumed, risking everything I had worked for all these years. But the alternative—letting Steven walk blindly into danger—was something I couldn't live with.

Taking a deep breath, I silently pushed the door open

and stepped inside. The interior was bright from the natural light pouring through the large window behind the desk—the window in front of which a familiar silhouette stood. The air smelled like men's cologne, like him, and for a moment, the ache in my chest tightened. It took everything in me to stay rooted where I stood and not rush to him, wrap my arms around him, and bury my face in his neck. I wanted to hold him, to breathe him in, to get lost in the warmth of him while the rest of the world kept spinning, forgotten.

But the world wouldn't wait, and neither could I. This was it. The moment of truth.

"Steven," I said softly, my voice barely above a whisper.

He turned slowly, his eyes widening in shock as they locked onto mine. For a moment, neither of us moved, the air between us thick with unspoken words, with the weight of everything we had lost.

"Alessandra?" His voice was filled with disbelief, as if he couldn't quite believe what he was seeing. "What are you doing here?"

I took a step forward, my heart aching at the confusion and pain in his eyes. "I could ask you the same thing," I replied, trying to keep my tone light, but the tremor in my voice betrayed me.

He shook his head, his expression hardening as he took a step back. "I'm doing my job," he said, his voice cold.

My stomach twisted at his words. "Steven, please... you don't know what you're getting yourself into."

His eyes narrowed, and I could see the determination there, the fire that had always driven him. "Then tell me," he said, his voice sharp. "Tell me what's going on. Tell me why you left, why you disappeared without a word. Or is it too complicated?" The mocking tone of his words cut deeply.

I had always wondered if this moment would come, had tried to prepare myself for it. But now, standing here in front of him, the weight of the truth was almost too much to bear.

I wanted to tell him everything—to explain the deals, the danger, the blood we both had on our hands. But saying it out loud would make it real, and I wasn't sure either of us could handle that.

"I left because I had to," I said, my voice shaking. "I left because it was the only way to protect you."

"Protect me?" He laughed, a bitter sound that cut through the tension in the room. "From what, Alessandra? From you? From your family?"

Tears welled in my eyes, but I blinked them back, refusing to let them fall. "Yes," I whispered. "From them. From me. From a life that would have destroyed us both."

For a moment, Steven just stared at me, his expression unreadable. Then he shook his head, his jaw clenched in anger and frustration. "You shouldn't have made that decision for me," he said, his voice tight. "You shouldn't get to decide what I can or can't handle."

"I know," I said, my voice breaking. "I know. But I couldn't bear the thought of losing you. And if anything had ever happened to you... I thought I was doing the right thing."

"And now?" he asked, his eyes searching mine. "What about now, Alessandra?"

Now. The word hung in the air between us, heavy with possibilities, with choices that could change everything.

"Now..." I took a deep breath, forcing myself to meet his gaze. "Now I'm here to warn you. You need to stop, Steven.

You need to walk away from this investigation before it's too late."

He stared at me, his eyes filled with a mix of anger and confusion. "And if I don't?" he asked, his voice low.

I wanted to tell him more—to explain that the Navarra family didn't just bury secrets; they buried people who found them. But my throat tightened, and all I could say was: "Then I don't know what will happen," I admitted, the fear evident in my voice. "But I do know that if you keep pursuing this, you're going to find yourself in a world of trouble. And I won't be able to protect you."

The silence between us stretched, thick and suffocating. His eyes locked on mine, searching for something—maybe an answer, or maybe just a reason to trust me again.

I had nothing to offer him. Just this warning and a heart that still bled for him.

For a long moment, Steven said nothing, his eyes locked onto mine as he weighed his options, as he tried to make sense of everything I had told him.

I wanted to warn him about more, but even I wasn't sure which shadow would strike first—my family, or the truth he was so determined to find.

Chapter 37

A Point of No Return

Steven

The hum of a newsroom was a steady rhythm that I had grown accustomed to over the years. Today, however, it was a distraction and I couldn't afford distractions right now. There was a nagging sense of unease in the back of my mind, something I couldn't quite shake. So I'd holed up in my office and closed the door—something I rarely did.

I was staring out the window thinking through the latest documents I had uncovered, the threads of the investigation slowly weaving together into a larger, more dangerous picture when the sound of my name pulled me from my thoughts.

I turned, expecting to see a colleague or my editor with another lead. Instead, my heart nearly stopped when I realized who it was.

Alessandra.

She was standing in my office directly in front of me. For a moment, time seemed to freeze. The years that had passed without her melted away, leaving only the memory of the woman I had loved—the woman who had left me without a word.

I remembered everything, every moment, every conversation about the future we'd never have. The memories evaporated, replaced by the cold reality of the woman standing in front of me now—the woman who had taken that future and left it in pieces.

"Steven," was all she said, her voice soft yet carrying a weight that made the air in the room feel heavy.

My pulse thrummed in my ears, drowning out the faint hum of the newsroom. My knuckles whitened as I gripped the edge of the desk, as if bracing for impact. "Alessandra," I replied, the shock evident in my voice. "What are you doing here?"

I could feel the tension radiating off her, see the secrets in her eyes—the same eyes that had once looked at me like I was her whole world. She was as beautiful as ever, but that beauty was no longer comforting. It was dangerous now, wrapped in mystery and the shadows of the life she had never let me see. My mind raced, trying to piece together why she was here now, after all this time. The last time I saw her, she had disappeared without a trace, leaving me with nothing but questions and an aching heart.

She began trying to explain herself, her words a tangled web of justification, all circling back to one central theme: she had left to protect me. Every action she had taken, every lie she had told, was done with my safety in mind. But as I stood there, the anger that had simmered inside me for years began to bubble to the surface.

She kept talking, her voice trembling slightly, as if she genuinely felt sympathy for me because of what she was saying. But the more she spoke, the more the knot of frustration tightened in my chest.

Her words blurred in my ears. I wasn't here—I was back in the apartment the night I found her side of the bed empty, her closet stripped bare. No explanation, no answers —just the silence she left behind.

I shook my head, frustration and anger coiling tightly inside me. "You shouldn't have made that decision for me," I said, my voice sharp, barely controlled. "You shouldn't get to decide what I can or can't handle."

Her eyes shimmered with unshed tears, and her voice trembled as she spoke. "I know," she said, the words catching in her throat. "I know. But I couldn't bear the thought of losing you. And if anything had ever happened to you... I thought I was doing the right thing."

I felt the sting of her words, the weight of the years between us pressing down on my chest. "And now?" I demanded, searching her face for answers. "What about now, Alessandra?"

She hesitated, taking a deep breath before finally meeting my gaze. "Now..." Her voice wavered, but she forced herself to keep going. "Now I'm here to warn you. You need to stop, Steven. You need to walk away from this investigation before it's too late."

I stared at her, torn between the anger burning in my chest and the confusion gnawing at the edges of my resolve. "And if I don't?" I asked, the words coming out low, almost a whisper.

Her face softened, and I could see the fear behind her eyes. "Then I don't know what will happen," she said, her voice laced with a vulnerability I hadn't seen in years. "But I do know that if you keep pursuing this, you're going to find yourself in a world of trouble. And I won't be able to protect you."

I stared at her, the words hanging heavy between us. She wanted me to walk away, to turn my back on everything I'd been working toward, everything that had hunted me since the day she left. But how could I? How could I abandon the truth, especially now that I was so close to it? Especially now that I understood what had really happened —what had driven her away from me in the first place?

"You're asking me to stop," I said slowly, my voice hardening with each word. "But this isn't just about you anymore, Alessandra. It's about the truth. It's about exposing the darkness that's been hiding in plain sight, the kind of darkness that destroyed what we had. You want me to give that up?"

Her eyes flickered with something I couldn't quite place —regret, maybe, or something deeper. "Steven, you don't understand—"

"No," I interrupted, my frustration boiling over. I stepped closer, the space between us shrinking to the point I could touch her if I barely lifted my arm. But I didn't and I wouldn't. Instead, my hands were clenched in fists at my sides.

"You didn't trust me then, and you don't trust me now," I said, my voice low but sharp. " You left me in the dark, and now you want me to just walk away? To pretend like none of this ever happened? No. You don't get to show up after all these years and expect me to walk away just because you told me to."

She flinched at my words, but I didn't stop. I couldn't.

"I could have saved you," I continued, my voice rising. "If you'd just trusted me, we could have fought this together. But now? Now I'm going to save myself. I'm going to expose the truth, and I'm not going to stop just because you showed up after all these years and told me to."

A silence fell between us, thick and suffocating. Alessandra's face hardened, the vulnerability I'd seen a moment ago vanishing, replaced by the cold, calculating exterior I remembered from the past.

"You think you can handle this, Steven?" she said, her voice low, a dangerous edge creeping into it. "You think you know what you're dealing with? You have no idea what exists in the darkness. You have no idea what you're up against."

"Then tell me," I challenged, stepping closer, refusing to back down. "Tell me what's so terrifying that you had to disappear, that you had to destroy everything we had."

She shook her head slowly, a bitter smile playing on her lips. "It's not that simple," she murmured, her tone almost pitying. "This isn't a game, Steven. You're poking at something that can't be fixed with a well-written article or an exposé. This is a world where the rules don't apply, where there are no limits to what people will do to protect their power. If you keep pushing, if you keep prodding, you're going to find yourself in the middle of something you can't escape."

I clenched my jaw, every instinct in me screaming to keep going, to press for more answers. But I could see it. Even with the schooled expression and the clothes that screamed wealth and power, I could see the fear in her eyes, the way her hands trembled slightly at her sides. She was terrified—for me, or for herself, I wasn't sure. But it was there. And it should have been a reminder of the danger I was stepping into.

"So what do you want me to do, Alessandra?" I asked, my voice quieter now, but no less resolute. "Just walk away?

Forget everything I've uncovered, everything I've been working toward?"

She looked at me, her eyes softening for just a moment before the mask slipped back into place. "I want you to be safe," she said simply. "I want you to live. But if you keep going down this path, you won't have that choice for much longer."

I took a deep breath, the weight of her words settling over me. I knew she was right—at least, in part. I knew he deeper I went, the more dangerous this investigation would become.

For a moment, her words chipped away at my resolve. But then I remembered the nights I spent waiting for answers that never came, the years of chasing shadows she left behind. No, I couldn't stop now. Not for her. Not for anyone.

"I'm not stopping," I said finally, my voice firm. "I'm going to see this through, no matter what it takes."

Alessandra's eyes flashed with something—anger, fear, maybe both. She opened her mouth to say something, but then closed it, her expression hardening once more.

"Then there's nothing more I can do for you," she said, her voice cold, distant. "I warned you, Steven. I came here to try and save you, but if you're determined to throw yourself into the fire, I can't stop you."

Her voice wavered, and for a second, I felt my own resolve waver. But I remembered the nights spent piecing together the trail she left behind, the sleepless hours trying to make sense of her disappearance.

She turned to leave, her back straight, her movements precise and controlled. But just before she reached the door, she paused, her hand resting on the handle.

"Be careful, Steven," she said, her voice softer now,

almost a whisper. "The truth might not be what you're expecting. And once you find it... there's no going back."

Without another word, she opened the door and slipped out, leaving me alone in the room, the echoes of our conversation lingering in the air. I stood there for a long time, staring at the door she had just walked through, my mind racing with everything she had said, everything she hadn't said.

I knew I was in over my head. I knew there were risks. But as I sat back down at my desk, staring at the documents spread out before me, I also knew that I couldn't turn back now. Not after everything I'd learned. Not after seeing her again.

The truth was out there, waiting to be uncovered. And no matter what Alessandra said, no matter how dangerous it might be, I was going to find it. I had to.

There was no other choice.

Chapter 38

Old Feelings, New Problems

Alessandra

My thoughts were consumed with Steven—his voice, his anger, the way his eyes had burned with a mixture of pain and determination. Seeing him again had been like walking into a warm room except you were coming inside from a summer day. In a different time, a different place, the warmth would have been appreciated. Instead, it had been nearly suffocating. My skin prickled with the memory of his gaze, and no matter how hard I tried, I couldn't shake the sensation of his presence clinging to me.

I shouldn't have gone to him. I knew that the moment I saw his face, the way he looked at me with a mixture of disbelief and hurt, the emotions I'd tried so hard to bury surged back to the surface. It took everything in me to keep my composure, to warn him without falling apart.

Yes, I had left him to protect him, to keep him from the darkness that surrounded my family. Now, however, all I had done was push him further into it. The irony was cruel and bitter, like a knife twisted in my chest.

When I reached the estate, I forced myself to take a deep breath, steeling myself for the confrontation I knew was coming. My father would already know about my visit to Steven—there were no secrets in our world, no moves that went unnoticed. I had been informed about Steven's investigation only after my father's informant had briefed him. It was a clear reminder that I was never fully in control, not when it came to my family. They were always one step ahead, always watching, waiting for any sign of weakness.

I stepped out of the car and walked up the stone steps, the weight of my choices pressing down on me with each step. The door opened before I could reach it, a silent signal that I was expected. The staff didn't make eye contact as I passed; they knew better than to acknowledge the tension that clung to the air like a thick fog.

"Miss Navarra," a soft voice called as I passed the grand foyer. Dr. Marconi was waiting for me near the staircase, his gray hair slightly disheveled, his coat partially unbuttoned. He held a clipboard against his chest, as though weighing whether or not to speak.

I paused. "Is something wrong?"

He gave me a small, patient smile. "Not at all. I just finished with your father." He flipped through his notes, glancing at one particular page. "His recovery is progressing. Blood pressure is stable, and his energy is returning."

I exhaled, some of the tension easing from my shoulders—but only slightly. My father's health had been a concern lately, and while the news was good, I knew that a healthy Lorenzo Navarra was more dangerous than a weakened one.

"Thank you, Doctor," I said, my tone polite but distant.

"I told him to avoid stress." The doctor chuckled. "But you know how he is."

"Yes," I replied, my lips tightening into a thin line. "I do."

The doctor offered a small nod and left. But his words echoed in my mind as I ascended the stairs. Avoid stress. My father lived on stress. It fueled him, sharpened him. And now, here I was, about to add even more to his plate.

Inside, the house was as grand and imposing as ever, its opulence a stark contrast to the turmoil churning inside me. My father was waiting in his study, his back to me as he stared out the window. The room was dimly lit, the only light coming from the flickering flames in the fireplace. The scent of burning wood filled the air, mingling with the faint smell of his cologne.

"Alessandra," he said without turning around, his voice low, measured. "I was beginning to wonder when you'd return."

"I had to see him," I replied, my voice steady despite the turmoil within me. "I had to deliver a warning."

He turned then, his eyes sharp, calculating. "A warning? Or did you go to make yourself feel better?"

I met his gaze, refusing to back down. "If he keeps digging, he'll uncover things that could put him in danger—and us. I let him know that he should stop or there would be consequences."

A flicker of something passed through his eyes—annoyance, perhaps, or something darker. "He's a journalist, Alessandra. Digging is what they do. It's in his nature. You knew this when you were with him. How did he take your warning?" He asked with a hint of mocking in his tone.

I learned a long time ago it was best to say what I wanted, but to maintain emotional neutrality when it came to my father. I told him the truth. "He said I couldn't stop him."

"And what do you propose we do?" my father asked, his tone almost bored. "Eliminate him?"

The coldness of his suggestion sent a shiver down my spine. "No," I said quickly, the word sharper than I intended. "I'll handle it. I'll make sure he backs off."

My father studied me for a long moment, his expression unreadable. "You're still in love with him," he said finally, his voice soft, almost pitying. "After all these years, after everything, you still care."

I didn't respond. There was no point in denying it. He had always been able to read me, even when I tried to hide my feelings. The silence stretched between us, heavy and suffocating.

"Love makes you weak, Alessandra," he continued, his voice growing harder. "It clouds your judgment, makes you vulnerable. You can't afford that in our world."

"I know," I said, my voice barely above a whisper. "But I can't let anything happen to him. I'll find a way to protect him without compromising us."

"And if you can't?" he asked, raising an eyebrow. "If he refuses to back down?"

I swallowed hard, the weight of the question pressing down on me like a stone. "Then I'll do what needs to be done," I said, forcing the words out. "I'll do whatever it takes to protect the family."

My father nodded, satisfied with my response. "See that you do," he said, turning back to the window. "But remember, Alessandra—there are no half-measures in our world. You're either in or you're out."

I turned to leave, my mind racing with the implications of his words. As I reached the door, he spoke again, his voice low and cold. "And Alessandra... if you can't handle it, someone else will."

The threat hung in the air, a reminder of the consequences of failure. I nodded once, not trusting myself to speak, and left the room.

As I walked down the long corridor, the walls closing in around me, I felt the weight of my choices pressing down on me. I had never stopped loving Steven, but that love had become a curse, a chain that bound me to a world I despised. And now, I was caught between two impossible choices—protect the man I loved once again or betray the family that had raised me.

I reached the sanctuary of my room, the only place in this house where I could let my guard down. But even here, I couldn't escape the reality of what I was facing. I had made my decision long ago, but the cost of that decision was becoming clearer with each passing day.

I couldn't let Steven go. I couldn't let him destroy himself in his quest for the truth. But protecting him meant betraying everything I had been raised to value, everything I had fought to protect.

As I sat down at the edge of my bed, my hands trembling, I knew that whatever path I chose, there would be no turning back. The darkness that surrounded me was closing in, and I was running out of time to find a way out.

The only thing I knew for certain was that I couldn't lose Steven again. Not like this. Not when the stakes were higher than ever.

But to protect him, I would have to walk a very dangerous line—a line that, once crossed, could never be undone.

And that was the most terrifying truth of all.

Part Three

The Rising Stakes

Chapter 39

The New Lead

Steven

I leaned back in my chair, staring at the cork-board in front of me, which was now covered with a web of photographs, documents, and sticky notes—each one representing a piece of the puzzle I was trying to solve. The deeper I dug, the more complicated the picture became, and the more dangerous the stakes felt.

It had been days since my encounter with Alessandra, but her words still echoed in my mind, a constant reminder of the risks I was taking. She had tried to warn me, to steer me away from the path I was on, but I couldn't—wouldn't—listen. The truth was out there, waiting to be uncovered, and I was too close to back down now.

My phone buzzed on the desk, snapping me out of my thoughts. I picked it up, seeing an unknown number flashing on the screen. A part of me hesitated, the memory of past threats lingering in the back of my mind, but my curiosity won out. I swiped to answer.

"Porter," I said, my voice steady.

There was a brief pause, then a low, distorted voice came through the line. "If you want to know the truth, follow the money. Tucker isn't who he seems. Start with his donors."

The line went dead before I could ask any questions, the sound of the dial tone filling my ear. I stared at the phone for a moment. We got tips called in all the time from informants but I hadn't put feelers out for this one. I'd tried to keep my story under wraps as much as possible to avoid anyone getting caught in crossfire. My gut told me this wasn't just a random call.

Quickly, I jotted down the details of the call and began searching for information on the politician the voice had mentioned. It didn't take long to uncover a list of his top donors—corporations, wealthy individuals, all names that were familiar in the circles of power. But one name stood out, one that hadn't been on my radar before: a shell corporation with ties to a prominent New York businessman. A businessman who, as it turned out, had connections to the Navarra family.

I felt a surge of adrenaline as the pieces began to fall into place. Money laundering, political influence, and now a direct link to one of the most powerful crime families in the city. This was it—this was the story I'd been searching for.

But with that excitement came a sense of unease. I knew the Navarra family was dangerous—more dangerous than anything I'd ever dealt with before. And now, I was poking around in their business, hoping to bring their secrets to the light. It was a risk, a big one, but I couldn't stop now. The truth had to come out, no matter the cost.

As I stared at the connections forming on the board, an idea began to take shape. I knew I was getting in over my head, but there was one person who might be able to help—

my brother, Nate. He'd always been the resourceful one, the one with the answers when I didn't even know what the questions were. And with his position in the FBI, he had access to information that could make or break this story.

I picked up my phone and dialed his number. He answered on the second ring.

"Steven? Everything okay?" Nate's voice was calm, but I could hear the undercurrent of concern. I rarely called him during the day.

"Yeah, I'm fine," I replied quickly, not wanting to alarm him. "But I need a favor."

There was a pause on the other end, the kind that came when Nate was weighing the situation before responding. "What kind of favor?"

"I'm looking into a politician," I began, choosing my words carefully. "Got an anonymous tip this morning that led me to one of his top donors. Turns out the donor's connected to a shell corporation with ties to... let's just say some very powerful people in New York."

"Powerful people?" Nate's tone shifted, growing more serious. "What are you getting yourself into, Steven?"

"Nothing I can't handle," I said, though I wasn't entirely sure that was true. "I just need you to run a quick check for me. See what you can find on this shell corporation. I don't have much—just a name and some basic info—but it's tied to a businessman who might be laundering money for these... powerful people."

Nate didn't respond right away. I could almost hear the gears turning in his head, weighing the risks against the potential benefits. Finally, he spoke. "Steven, you know I can't officially get involved in anything that isn't part of an official investigation."

"I know," I cut in, trying to sound nonchalant. "I'm not

asking for anything official. Just a favor, from one brother to another. I need to know if this lead is worth following, or if I'm chasing my tail here."

There was another pause, and I could tell Nate was torn. "This is serious, isn't it?"

"Yeah," I admitted, the weight of the investigation pressing down on me. "It is."

"Alright, tell me what you're looking for," Nate finally said, his voice resigned.

I gave him the highlights.

"I'll see what I can find. But, Steven—be careful. If these people are who I think they are, you're playing with fire."

I almost laughed. Nate had been warning me about playing with fire since we were kids—like when I climbed the old treehouse in our backyard and almost broke my arm. He had pulled me down then, and now he was trying to do the same. But I wasn't a kid anymore.

"Thanks, Nate. I owe you one."

"You owe me more than one," he replied, his tone lightening just a bit. "I'll get back to you as soon as I can. And Steven... if things start to get out of hand, you call me. Don't try to handle anything dangerous on your own."

"I will," I promised, though we both knew it was a promise I might not keep.

As I hung up the phone, I felt a mix of relief and anxiety. Nate was my safety net, the one person I could trust to have my back no matter what. But I also knew that involving him came with risks—risks I wasn't sure I wanted to take, but wasn't sure what other choice I had. The deeper I got into this investigation, the more I realized how dangerous it was becoming. But I couldn't stop now. I was too close to the truth, and the truth needed to come out, no matter the cost.

This was bigger than both of us, bigger than anything I had ever faced before. And no matter what it took, I was going to see it through to the end.

Because the truth needed to be exposed. And I was the only one who could do it.

Later that day, I met up with Doug Melon, a fellow journalist who had been covering corruption in New York for years. We sat at a small coffeehouse, our conversation kept low as we discussed the latest developments in our respective investigations. I trusted Doug—he was one of the few people who understood the drive that pushed me forward, even when the risks were high.

"So, what's new on your end?" Doug asked, taking a sip of his coffee.

I glanced around, ensuring we weren't being overheard, then leaned in. "I got a tip this morning," I said, keeping my voice low. "About a politician—turns out his top donor has ties to the Navarra family."

Doug's expression darkened. "The Navarras?" he repeated, his tone wary. "Steven, you need to be careful. Those people are brutal. If they catch wind of what you're doing..."

"I know," I interrupted, my voice firm. "But I'm not backing down. This is too big to ignore."

Doug sighed, leaning back in his chair. "Just... watch your back, okay? I've heard stories about people who've crossed them, and they don't end well."

I nodded, appreciating his concern but knowing there was no turning back now. "I will," I promised. "But I have to see this through. There's more at stake here than just a story."

Doug studied me for a moment, then nodded slowly. "Let me know if you need anything."

I gave him a small smile. "Thanks, I'll do that."

As I left the coffeehouse and made my way back to the office, I felt the weight of the investigation pressing down on me. The excitement of uncovering the truth was still there, but it was tempered by a growing sense of dread. The Navarra family was a powerful force, and I knew I was walking a fine line. One wrong move, and everything could come crashing down.

But despite the risks, despite the warnings, I couldn't stop. The truth was out there, buried beneath layers of deception and corruption, and I was determined to bring it to light. Even if it meant facing the darkness head-on.

Back at the office, I started connecting the dots between the money laundering operation and the Navarra family. The more I uncovered, the clearer the picture became. This wasn't just about a corrupt politician—this was about power, control, and a web of influence that stretched far beyond what I had imagined.

As the day turned into night, the newsroom emptied out, leaving me alone with my thoughts and the evidence spread out before me. My mind kept drifting back to Alessandra, to the warning she had given me, and the fear in her eyes. It wasn't just fear of what I'd uncover—it was fear of what the Navarras would do once I uncovered it. She had lived among them. She knew what they were capable of. And honestly, that terrified me more than anything.

This was bigger than both of us, bigger than anything I had ever faced before. And no matter what it took, I was going to see it through to the end.

Because the truth needed to be exposed. And I was the only one who could do it.

Chapter 40

Follow the Money

Steven

"*If you want to know the truth, follow the money.*"

That was easier said than done. Campaign finance was a labyrinth, designed to obscure the true sources of funds behind layers of PACs, shell corporations, and individual donors who were anything but ordinary citizens. But I wasn't new to this game. I knew how to navigate the maze, how to peel back the layers until I found what I was looking for.

I'd started with the campaign finance reports, combing through the list of donors. Most of the names were familiar —local businesses, wealthy benefactors, and the occasional celebrity looking to curry favor. But one name had stood out: Crossroads Consulting, LLC.

Something about it nagged at me, a faint tickle at the back of my mind that told me to dig deeper. So I did.

A few quick searches revealed that Crossroads Consulting was registered as a consulting firm, but there was little information available about its operations. The company had no website, no online presence beyond a generic homepage, and its listed address was a P.O. box in an upscale Manhattan neighborhood. Red flags, all of them.

Next, I turned my attention to the owner of Crossroads Consulting—one Leonard P. Cross. He wasn't a public figure, at least not in the traditional sense. But after some digging, I found that he was linked to several other shell companies, all of which had made significant donations to Tucker's campaign over the years. The pattern was clear: this was a front, a way to funnel money into the campaign without drawing too much attention.

But where was the money coming from? That was the question. Actually it was a multimillion-dollar question.

I'd spent the better part of the last few days holed up in my office, poring over Senator Harold Tucker's financials. The connection between Tucker and the Navarras was clearer, but I needed more—a smoking gun that tied them together without a doubt. And I felt like Cross was it.

That's when my phone rang, Nate's name flashing on the screen.

It had been three days since I'd asked for his help, and I could tell by the sound of his voice that he'd found something. "Steven, we need to talk."

My pulse quickened. "What did you find?"

"You were right. Crossroads Consulting is a front—it's connected to a series of offshore accounts, most of them tied to organized crime. And Steven, this isn't small-time stuff. The kind of money moving through these accounts... it's huge. Tens of millions. I don't think I have to tell you who you're up against here."

I leaned back in my chair, the weight of Nate's words sinking in. "Navarras?"

"Yeah. And that's not all. The politician you're looking into—Tucker? He's dirty, Steven. Really dirty. There are payments, backdoor deals, favors... You name it, it's in there. The guy's got to be connected to the Navarras." Nate sounded frustrated when he added on under his breath, "I don't know why we haven't gone after all of these guys sooner."

I felt a surge of excitement. "This is it, Nate. This is exactly the bombshell I've been looking for."

Nate didn't respond right away. When he did, his voice was more serious than I'd ever heard it. "Steven, you need to back off. This is bigger than anything you've dealt with before. The Navarras don't play games, and Tucker's a powerful guy. They won't hesitate to take you out if they feel cornered. You need to let the authorities handle this."

I ran a hand through my hair, already knowing what I was going to say, but hating that I had to say it. "I can't stop, Nate. I'm too far in, and the story's too important. If I back off now, they'll keep getting away with it. This is my chance to expose them."

"Steven," Nate's voice had an edge to it now, "this isn't just about a story anymore. It's your life. I get it, I really do, but you're not equipped to handle what happens next if something like this goes sideways."

I sat up, my jaw tightening. "I can handle it. I've been in plenty of dangerous situations before."

"Handling it is one thing, surviving it is another. Look, I've given you what I can. Just... stay smart, alright? Call me if you need anything."

His words hung in the air between us, heavy with meaning. Nate was crossing a line just giving me this information, and we both knew it. I could feel the weight of his warning, the gravity of what I was about to do.

"There's one more thing," Nate said, his tone grave. "Tucker's campaign knows someone's sniffing around the financials. If you don't wrap this up soon, they'll start covering their tracks even better—and when they do, it'll be like trying to catch smoke."

"Thanks, Nate."

"Yeah," he sighed, "don't make me regret this. And Steven? Stay safe."

"I will."

As I hung up, I stared at the cork-board in front of me, the web of connections staring back like a taunt. Nate had given me enough to put Tucker's entire career—and maybe his life—in jeopardy. But more than that, he'd confirmed what I already knew: the Navarras were at the center of this.

My mind was racing, but one thought kept pushing through: What would this mean for Alessandra? Could I really go through with this, knowing that it would destroy her family—and possibly her, too? But I shook it off. There was no turning back now.

I decided to dig deeper into the financials of Crossroads' CEO, Leonard Cross. It wasn't easy—accessing those kinds of records took time and finesse, not to mention a few favors called in from contacts who owed me. But when the reports finally landed in my inbox, what I found made my stomach tighten.

The money flowing into Crossroads Consulting wasn't just coming from Tucker's wealthy supporters. It was coming from offshore accounts in the Cayman Islands, from businesses with ties to organized crime, and most damning of all, from companies linked to the Navarra family. The same family I'd been investigating for months.

I leaned back in my chair. I let the idea of the size of the discovery which was both exciting and daunting, wash over me. This wasn't just about campaign finance violations—this was a full-blown conspiracy, one that practically connected Senator Tucker to the darkest elements of New York's underworld. And if the Navarras were involved, then this was bigger than anything I'd anticipated.

The next step was to confirm the connection, to find the smoking gun that would tie Tucker to the Navarras beyond a shadow of a doubt. That meant tracking the money back to its source, figuring out who was pulling the strings behind the scenes.

I had spent hours looking through financial records, tracing the flow of funds from one shell company to another, trying to untangle the web of transactions designed to confuse and obfuscate. It was tedious work, the kind that made your eyes burn and your head throb, but I was used to it. And eventually, my persistence paid off.

The breakthrough came when I found a series of wire transfers from an account in the Cayman Islands to a New York-based law firm—Harrison & Whitman. The firm's partners were well-known for their connections to powerful people in the city, and one name in particular stood out: Victor Whitman.

When I saw Whitman's name in the transaction log, my pulse spiked. I leaned forward, scanning the wire transfers again to make sure my eyes weren't deceiving me. Whitman. The fixer. The man who cleaned up scandals before they ever hit the front page.

The money trail was clear: Crossroads Consulting funneled funds through offshore accounts, which eventually made their way to Whitman. And Whitman's role? He wasn't just a middleman. He was the bridge between Senator Tucker's dirty campaign and the Navarras' illicit empire. Whitman didn't just clean up messes—he orchestrated cover-ups, paid off insiders, and ensured everything stayed buried. He'd represented corrupt politicians, mob bosses, and anyone else who could afford him. And now, he was the key to exposing them all.

The wire transfers were significant—hundreds of thousands of dollars, all funneled through layers of transactions before landing in Whitman's hands. But they didn't stop there. Further digging revealed that Whitman wasn't just protecting Tucker; he was also protecting the Navarras, acting as a legal and financial shield to keep their operations under the radar.

My heart pounded as I connected the final dots. Crossroads Consulting was a front for funneling Navarra money to Tucker's campaign, and Whitman was the linchpin holding it all together. Without him, the whole operation would unravel.

For a moment, I sat back, the weight of the discovery pressing down on me. This wasn't just a single breadcrumb. This was a trail of them that could bring everything crashing down—Tucker, the Navarras, and anyone else tangled in their web of corruption. But it also meant I was about to put a target on my back. If they knew how close I was, I'd be in more danger than ever.

And then there was Alessandra. I could still see the way her eyes had softened when she warned me, as if she wanted to say something more but couldn't. An ache formed deep in my chest. Was she in danger? Could I save her if she was? I ran a hand down my face, trying to push thoughts of her away.

I wanted answers. I wanted to hear her say she didn't

know how far her family's reach went, that she wasn't part of this. But what if she did know? What if she was keeping secrets bigger than I could handle?

Just because I wanted to, I realized I wasn't ready to know the answer. Not yet.

Chapter 41

A Smoking Gun

Steven

I navigated the bustling streets of Manhattan, my mind racing with everything Nate had revealed. The deeper I dug, the darker the shadows became, but this was it—the moment I'd been waiting for. The dots were finally connecting, and all roads led to Victor Whitman.

Whitman's office was the key. If I could get in and find the documents tying him to Cross, the Navarras, and Tucker, I'd have the smoking gun I needed to blow this story wide open.

I'd done my homework. Whitman's law firm was housed in a sleek high-rise in the heart of Manhattan—a fortress of glass and steel. The kind of place designed to keep secrets safe. But I knew how to navigate places like this.

As an investigative journalist, you learn fast that not everything is handed to you through official channels. Public records can only take you so far. Sometimes, if you want the truth, you have to step off the legal path and get your hands a little dirty and hope you don't get caught.

You're not building a case for a courtroom—you're building one for society, for the court of public opinion, where the truth matters more than the technicalities. Over the years, I'd picked up plenty of tricks—some from sources who owed me favors, others from experience in the field.

As I circled the block, I checked my phone for the security feed I'd hacked earlier. The back delivery entrance was clear. I adjusted the cap on my head, shoved my hands in my pockets, and walked briskly to the alley, slipping between shadows. I glanced around before swiping a borrowed keycard across the panel by the delivery door. The light blinked green, and the lock clicked.

Inside, the narrow hallway was dim and industrial—concrete walls, exposed pipes, and the faint hum of machinery. The main office floors were several stories up, but the elevator required a key card so the stairs would have to do.

I climbed quickly, my breath steady despite the pounding of my heart. On the fifteenth floor, I cracked open the door to the hallway and listened. Silence, except for the distant hum of the building's ventilation. Perfect.

Whitman's office was at the far end of the corridor, marked by a polished brass plaque. I reached into my bag, pulling out a compact electronic lock pick. The lock was high-end, but I'd handled worse. After a few tense minutes, the mechanism clicked, and the door swung open.

Inside, the office smelled like leather and old paper. Sleek bookshelves lined the walls, and a massive mahogany desk sat in front of a floor-to-ceiling window overlooking the city. But I wasn't here to admire the view.

I adjust my gloves and moved quickly. First, I placed the hard drive cloner next to the computer on Whitman's desk, connecting the cables and activating the device. The screen flickered to life as the cloner began copying every file on the drive. While it worked, I turned my attention to the filing cabinets.

Paper files could be just as valuable as digital ones. People tended to leave things off computers when they didn't want a digital trail. My fingers skimmed over the labels until I found the drawer I was looking for: Crossroads Consulting.

I yanked it open, flipping through contracts, invoices, and bank statements. My breath caught when I spotted a handwritten note from Lorenzo Navarra himself, detailing payments and instructions to Whitman. I quickly snapped photos of the documents with my phone, making sure to capture every detail.

The hard drive cloner beeped softly, signaling that it was finished. I disconnected it, slipped it into my bag, and carefully closed the file drawer. As I took one last glance around the office, my pulse quickened. This was the kind of evidence that could bring down everyone involved.

But then I heard it—footsteps in the hallway.

I killed the computer monitor and pressed myself against the wall in a dark corner, my breath shallow, my heart pounding. The footsteps grew louder, stopping right outside the door. I clenched my jaw, every muscle in my body tensed. *Don't open the door. Please, don't open the door.*

A shadow flickered beneath the crack, and I held my breath, praying whoever it was would move on. After what felt like an eternity, the footsteps continued down the hallway, fading into the distance.

I let out a shaky breath, wiping the sweat from my brow. That had been too close.

I opened the door cautiously, checking both directions before slipping into the hallway. My footsteps were light and quick as I made my way to the stairwell and out the door in which I came.

Once outside, the night air hit my face like a splash of water. I took a deep breath, trying to calm my racing heart. I had what I'd gone in search of but as I made my way back to my car, a nagging thought kept pulling at the edges of my mind: What would this mean for Alessandra?

She had warned me, tried to stop me, and I'd ignored her. Now, I was holding the evidence that could destroy her family.

The question wasn't whether I'd publish the story. I knew I would. The question was whether Alessandra would ever forgive me when I did and why did I care?

Chapter 42

Familial Pressure

Alessandra

The dining room was as imposing as ever, with its high ceilings, dark wood paneling, and a chandelier that cast a muted, almost haunting light over the long table. I had sat at this table countless times, surrounded by the most powerful members of the Navarra family, but tonight the air was thicker, charged with a tension I could feel in my bones.

My father sat at the head of the table, his expression a mask of calm authority. To anyone else, he would appear composed, in control. But I knew him better than anyone. I could see the slight tightening of his jaw, the way his fingers tapped rhythmically against the polished surface of the table—a subtle signal that something was deeply amiss.

As I took my seat, I caught a glance from Carlo—a long-time lieutenant in my father's circle. His gaze lingered a second too long, and a faint smirk tugged at the corner of his mouth, as if he knew more than he should. My stomach twisted. Carlo had always been a snake, loyal only to the power he could gain.

"There's been a development," Lorenzo began, his voice cutting through the silence like a knife. "Someone's been asking questions, getting too close to our operations. It's only a matter of time before they connect too many dots."

My heart pounded in my chest, but I kept my face neutral, giving nothing away. I glanced around the table at the others—men who had been part of this world far longer than I had, who knew the stakes better than anyone. Their expressions were a mix of concern and cold determination. They understood the gravity of what Lorenzo was saying.

"We cannot afford to have our businesses compromised," he continued, his eyes sweeping across the room, landing on me for just a fraction of a second longer than necessary. "This problem needs to be eliminated. Swiftly and without a trace."

My throat tightened, making it feel like I was swallowing glass, but I forced my breath to steady. He knew. Or at least, he suspected. But how much? How close was he to discovering the truth?

I had to speak, had to say something that would convince him I was still on his side, that I was handling the situation. "I've been monitoring the situation," I said, my voice steady despite the turmoil inside me. "It's under control. I believe we can neutralize the threat without drawing attention to ourselves."

Lorenzo's gaze sharpened, his eyes narrowing slightly as he studied me. "Neutralize?" he repeated, the word rolling off his tongue with a load of skepticism. "How do you propose we do that, Alessandra?"

I knew why he was doing this. We'd had this conversation in private. But putting it out there like this, it meant accountability for me. And accountability was the last thing I wanted right now because I didn't know exactly what I would do when the situation presented itself to make a choice.

I took a deep breath, carefully choosing my words. "We have resources, people who can make this disappear quietly. There's no need for drastic measures—not yet, at least. If we act too aggressively, it could backfire and bring even more scrutiny. Surely there are people he works with that know what he's working on. We can't take out every reporter on the block, though I know that would please you to no end, Father."

Lorenzo huffed as he leaned back in his chair, his fingers still drumming against the table. The silence stretched out, thick and suffocating. I could feel the weight of everyone's eyes moving between us, waiting for his verdict.

"And you're certain this is the best course of action?" he asked finally, his tone deceptively mild.

I met his gaze, refusing to let my fear show. "Yes. I'm confident that we can handle this without escalating the situation."

For a moment, he said nothing, just continued to watch me with that piercing gaze that always made me feel like he could see right through me. Then, slowly, he nodded. "Very well. But understand this, Alessandra—if you're wrong, if this situation spirals out of control, there will be consequences. Severe consequences."

The threat hung in the air, unspoken but clear. I forced myself to nod, my heart thudding in my chest. "I understand, Father."

The rest of the meeting passed in a blur, discussions of other business matters that I barely registered. All I could think about was Steven—how close he was to uncovering the truth, how much danger he was in. I had to find a way to stop him, to protect him, before it was too late.

As the meeting finally adjourned and the others began to file out of the room, Lorenzo caught my arm, pulling me aside. "Alessandra," he said, his voice low and laced with suspicion. "Are you hiding something from me?"

I looked up at him, forcing myself to hold his gaze, to keep my expression calm. "No, Father," I said softly. "I'm handling it."

He studied me for another long moment, his eyes searching mine. "I hope for your sake that's true," he murmured, releasing my arm. "Because if I find out you're lying to me..."

He didn't finish the sentence. He didn't need to. My imagination filled in the blanks—images of punishment, exile, or worse, flashing through my mind like lightning.

I nodded, my throat tight. "I won't let you down," I promised, hating the way the words felt like ash in my mouth.

He gave me a final, piercing look before turning and leaving the room. As soon as the sound of his footsteps faded, my knees buckled slightly, and I gripped the edge of the table to steady myself. My breaths came in shallow gasps, the weight of the encounter hitting me like a blow to the chest. The room spun for a moment, the oppressive walls closing in around me, but I forced myself to stand upright. Weakness wasn't an option—not here.

I had bought some time, but I knew it wasn't enough. Steven was in more danger than ever, and if I didn't act quickly, if I didn't find a way to steer him off this path, my father would find out the truth—and then, it wouldn't just be Steven's life on the line. It would be mine too.

But even as fear gripped me, another emotion surged to the surface—determination. I couldn't lose Steven again. Not like this. I would find a way to protect him, no matter the cost. Even if it meant going against everything I had been raised to believe, even if it meant betraying my family.

Because some things were worth risking everything for. And Steven was one of them.

But as I left the dining room and walked down the darkened hallway, a sense of dread settled over me, cold and unrelenting. Time was running out, and I could feel the noose tightening around both of us. I just didn't know if I could pull us out before it was too late.

Chapter 43

Revisiting the Past

Steven

The sound of pages turning echoed through the quiet room, each one a reminder of the promises I had made—and the ones I had broken many times over. The records room was a far cry from the chaos of the newsroom or the danger of the streets, but in its own way, it was just as daunting. The walls were lined with dusty shelves, their air thick with the smell of old paper and forgotten secrets.

I sat at one of the long tables, surrounded by stacks of records some of which I'd combed through dozens of times already, each one more damning than the last. The name "Navarra" was scrawled across so many of them, the ink faded but the implications as fresh as ever. The deeper I dug, the more my hands trembled, and the more the pit in my stomach grew.

Alessandra had warned me not to do this. She had pleaded with me to walk away, to leave the past buried where it belonged. But after everything that had happened

—the lies, the danger, the near-death escape in that alley—I couldn't stop. I had to know the truth, even if it meant betraying the trust we had once shared. Even if it meant confirming my worst fears.

The first file I opened was innocuous enough—a list of real estate holdings, a series of transactions that painted the Navarra family as savvy investors. But beneath the surface, there were hints of something darker. Properties bought under shell companies, funds moved through offshore accounts, connections to businesses that had long been rumored to be fronts for illegal activities. It was all there, buried under layers of legitimate business dealings, but unmistakable to anyone who knew where to look.

I pushed the file aside and reached for another, this one older, the pages yellowed with age. My fingers hesitated over the cover before I flipped it open.

A black-and-white photo of a man stared back at me, his features unmistakably similar to Alessandra's. Lorenzo Navarra, the patriarch of the Navarra family. The article that accompanied the photo was a piece of investigative journalism from the 1980s, detailing his rise to power in the criminal underworld, his ties to the Mafia, and his ruthless consolidation of power.

I felt a chill run down my spine as I read about the things he had done—the people he had crossed, the lives he had destroyed. This was the man who had raised Alessandra, who had shaped her into the woman she had become. The man who had torn her away from me.

I forced myself to keep reading, even as the words blurred on the page. The article went on to describe the Navarra family's influence over politicians, law enforcement, and even other crime families. It painted a picture of an empire built on fear and corruption, one that had thrived in the shadows for decades.

And then, buried deep in the article, I found it—her name.

Alessandra Navarra.

My breath hitched, and for a moment, the room seemed to tilt around me. I stared at the letters, as if seeing them in print would make them mean something different, something less damning.

It was just a brief mention, a single line in a paragraph about Lorenzo's family. Alessandra Navarra, his daughter, had been seen accompanying her father at various social events, always at his side, a poised and silent presence in the background. The reporter had speculated about her role in the family business, noting that she was rumored to be more than just a passive observer. There were whispers, unconfirmed but persistent, that she had been groomed from a young age to take on her father's legacy, to continue the Navarra dynasty.

My heart ached as I stared at her name, the letters swimming before my eyes. Alessandra had never told me the full truth about her family, but I had always wondered. Even in college, there had been signs—her reluctance to talk about her past, the way she would change the subject whenever her family came up, the distance she always kept between us when it came to that part of her life.

It was clear that Alessandra wasn't just someone caught in the orbit of her father's crimes—she was part of it. Whether by choice or by necessity, she had been involved in the very world I was now investigating, the world I was trying to expose.

A fresh wave of betrayal washed over me, bitter and cold. She had known all along. She had known what her family was, what they were capable of, and yet she had let me fall in love with her, had let me believe that we could have a future together. She had left me in the dark, kept me at arm's length, all while being part of something that could have destroyed us both.

But even as the anger built, there was something else—a deep, aching sadness that threatened to overwhelm me. Because no matter how much I wanted to hate her, no matter how much I wanted to blame her for everything, I couldn't shake the memories of the woman I had loved. The woman who had been kind and gentle, who had laughed with me, who had shared her dreams and fears. The woman who had left me because she believed it was the only way to protect me.

I closed the file, the sound of the pages snapping shut echoing in the quiet room. My hands were trembling, my heart pounding in my chest. I had come here looking for answers, and I had found them. But they weren't the answers I had wanted. They weren't the answers that would make this all easier to understand, to forgive.

I sat there for a long time, staring at the stack of files in front of me, the weight of the truth pressing down on me like a physical force. I had uncovered the past, the secrets that Alessandra had tried so hard to keep hidden. But in doing so, I had opened a door that couldn't be closed, had stepped into a world that was far more dangerous than I had ever imagined.

And now, I had to decide what to do with that knowledge.

Could I trust Alessandra? Could I believe that she had left me to protect me, that she hadn't been as deeply involved in her family's crimes as the documents suggested? Or was she just another pawn in her father's game, someone who had been forced into a role she hadn't wanted, but couldn't escape from?

I didn't know. And that uncertainty gnawed at me, ate away at the resolve I had built up over the years.

The only thing I knew for certain was that the truth was far more complicated than I had ever imagined. And that the deeper I went, the more dangerous it became—for both of us.

Chapter 44

A Final Warning

Alessandra

The night was quiet save for a gentle breeze rustling the leaves overhead as I waited in the shadows. I had chosen this spot carefully—a secluded park on the outskirts of the city, far from prying eyes and the reach of my family's influence. It was the kind of place that was supposed to feel safe, but tonight, it felt anything but.

My heart was pounding in my chest, each beat echoing the dread that had been building inside me since I made the decision to call Steven. I knew what I had to do, knew the words I needed to say, but the thought of facing him again, of seeing the anger and hurt in his eyes, made me want to run, to disappear back into the darkness where I belonged.

But I couldn't. Not this time.

I'd called his office and left a message with only a location, date, and time. And until now, I had no idea if he'd even show.

The crunch of footsteps on the gravel path pulled me from my thoughts, and I looked up to see Steven approaching, his silhouette barely visible in the dim light. For a moment, I just watched him, my heart aching at the sight. He moved with the same determined stride I remembered, his shoulders squared, his gaze fixed on me. There was no hesitation in his steps, no sign of the boyish flippancy he used to have. He had changed—hardened by the years, by the things he had seen and done. But so had I.

When he reached me, we stood there in silence, the weight of our past pressing down on us like a heavy shroud. His eyes searched mine, and I could see the conflict there, the mixture of emotions he was struggling to keep in check.

"What are we doing here, Alessandra?" he asked, his voice low, strained.

I took a deep breath, steeling myself for what was to come. "I had to warn you, Steven. You're in danger. Real danger. And I don't want you to get hurt because of me."

He scoffed, shaking his head as if trying to make sense of it all. "I've been in danger since the moment you walked into my life in that dorm stairwell. Don't pretend this is about protecting me. This is about you—about your family, and the mess you're tangled up in."

His words cut deep, but I forced myself to stay calm. He was right, of course. It was about my family, about the twisted web of power and corruption we had woven around ourselves. But it was about him too—about the man I had loved, still loved, and the danger he was walking into.

"I know you're angry," I said, my voice trembling despite my best efforts to steady it. "You have every right to be. But, Steven, you have to listen to me. If you keep digging, if you keep pushing... they will come for you. And when they do, there will be nothing I can do to stop them."

He crossed his arms over his chest, his jaw clenched in defiance. "And what about you, Alessandra? What role did you play in all of this? How deep are you in? Because from where I'm standing, it looks like you might be in just as much trouble as I am."

The accusation hung in the air between us, heavy and suffocating. I wanted to tell him the truth, to lay everything bare and let him see the full extent of the nightmare I had been living. But I couldn't. There were some truths too dangerous to speak aloud, some secrets that could never be shared.

"I've done what I had to do to survive," I said quietly, my voice barely above a whisper. "But that's not what this is about. This is about you, Steven. You need to leave New York. You need to get as far away from here as possible before it's too late."

He took a step closer, his eyes boring into mine, demanding answers I wasn't sure I could give. "And what if I don't? What if I can't just walk away? What if I need to know the truth, even if it destroys us both?"

The raw emotion in his voice nearly broke me.

"You can't save me, Steven," I said, my voice cracking under the weight of my emotions. "I'm already lost. But you... you can still walk away. You can still have a life—one that doesn't end in darkness."

He shook his head, his expression hardening. "No. You don't get to decide that for me again, Alessandra. You don't get to push me away and tell me it's for my own good. I'm not that kid you left behind anymore. I'm not afraid of the darkness."

Tears welled in my eyes, but I blinked them back, refusing to let them fall. "I never wanted to push you away," I whispered, the words catching in my throat. "But I had to. For your sake. For your safety. And now... now I'm begging you to listen to me. Please, Steven. If you ever loved me, if you ever cared about us, you'll leave. You'll forget about this investigation and walk away."

He stared at me, his eyes filled with a mixture of anger, pain, and determination. "I can't do that," he said, his voice resolute. "I've come too far, uncovered too much. I can't just walk away now. Not when I'm this close."

A tear slipped down my cheek, and I quickly wiped it away, my heart breaking at his words. I knew this would be the outcome, but hearing it, feeling the finality of it, was like a knife twisting in my chest.

"Then this might be the last time we see each other," I said, my voice barely a whisper.

He reached out, his hand brushing against mine, the touch sending a jolt of electricity through me. "It doesn't have to be," he said, his voice softening. "We could still—"

"No," I interrupted, pulling my hand away, the pain of the loss almost too much to bear. "There's no future for us, Steven. Not now. Not ever."

The words hung in the air, final and irrevocable. I turned away, unable to look at him any longer, knowing that if I did, I might not have the strength to walk away.

"Please," I said one last time, my back to him. "I'm begging you. Walk away."

Without waiting for his response, I started walking, each step tearing me further away from the man I had loved, from the life we could never have. I knew that by the time I reached the street, the tears I had been holding back would come, unstoppable and unrelenting. But for now, I kept walking, my heart breaking with every step.

Chapter 45

Not an Easy Decision

Steven

The walk back to my apartment passed in a haze, city lights smearing into streaks of neon and shadow as I replayed the conversation with Alessandra over and over in my mind. Her words echoed in my head, each one a dagger twisting in my gut. *You can't save me, Steven... You can still walk away... This might be the last time we see each other.*

I pushed open the door to my building and took the elevator to my apartment, my footsteps heavy with the weight of everything that had just happened. As I stepped inside, the familiar comfort of my home felt hollow, the quietness more oppressive than ever. I closed the door behind me, leaning against it as I tried to catch my breath, the reality of the situation crashing down on me like a wave.

The woman I had loved, the woman I still loved, had just told me to walk away. To leave everything behind and save myself. But how could I? How could I just turn my back on the investigation, on the truth I was so close to exposing? How could I ignore the corruption and darkness that had destroyed our relationship, that had driven us apart in the first place? And it was casting darkness over The City, the place I called home.

I moved to the couch, sinking into the cushions as I buried my face in my hands. My mind was a whirlwind of emotions—love, anger, confusion. I knew what she was asking of me. I understood why she was so desperate to protect me.

But if you keep going down this path, you won't have that choice for much longer. Her warning played on a loop in my head, the fear in her voice so raw and real that it made my chest tighten. I knew she was serious. I knew the danger was real. But did that mean I should just give up? Abandon everything I'd worked for, everything I believed in?

Leaving this investigation unfinished and walking away without the full truth being in the hands of the public, was not an option.

I stood up abruptly, pacing the length of my living room as my thoughts continued to spiral. I had always been driven by the truth, by the need to uncover it, no matter the cost. It was what had led me to journalism in the first place, what had fueled my career, my life. But now, that same drive was tearing me apart, pulling me in two different directions.

On one hand, there was Alessandra—my past, my love, my heart. She had sacrificed everything for my safety, and now she was asking me to do the same for myself. To walk away, to save myself, to leave her behind once and for all.

But on the other hand, there was the truth. The story. The corruption that had destroyed so many lives, that was still out there, festering in the shadows. If I walked away now, if I ignored everything I had uncovered, who else would be hurt? Who else would be destroyed by the Navarra family and their empire of secrets?

I stopped pacing, standing in the middle of the room as the conflict raged inside me. My heart and my head were at war, each one pulling me in a different direction, each one demanding a choice I wasn't sure I was ready to make.

Could I really walk away? Could I really abandon the story, the investigation, the truth? Could I live with myself if I did?

And then, there was Alessandra. The woman who had shattered my heart, who had left me in darkness, but who had also saved me from a life I couldn't understand. I had loved her once—loved her still, despite everything. But could I forgive her? Could I trust her? And if I did, what would that mean for the rest of my life? For the story I had been chasing for months?

I moved to the window, staring out at the city below, the lights twinkling like stars in the night. The world kept turning, kept moving, even as I stood here, frozen in indecision. But time was running out. The longer I waited, the more dangerous this investigation became—for both of us.

My phone buzzed on the coffee table, pulling me out of my thoughts. I hesitated for a moment before picking it up when I saw the name on the screen.

Jordan Mathis.

Jordan wasn't a friend, exactly, but he wasn't a stranger either. He was one of those contacts you develop over time in this line of work—someone who'd been useful once, and then useful again, until they became part of your network whether you liked them or not.

We'd crossed paths during an earlier investigation into police misconduct. He had been a reporter, too, but one who'd never played by the rules. He pushed limits, took risks most journalists wouldn't touch, and often bent the ethics of the job until they nearly snapped. The kind of guy who would burn a bridge if it meant getting the scoop.

Jordan's career had imploded after he got caught fabricating parts of a story—just enough to get headlines, but not enough to hold up under scrutiny. He'd gone from rising star to disgraced burnout practically overnight. But instead of disappearing, Jordan had adapted, using what he knew to stay useful. Whistleblowing, consulting, feeding reporters information that wasn't always clean but often led somewhere real.

He was resourceful, and he knew how the system worked from the inside out. That's why I trusted him, to a degree. He always knew where the skeletons were buried, because half the time, he'd helped bury them.

I answered the call, my voice steady despite the turmoil inside me.

"Steven," Jordan said, his voice low and urgent. "I've got something for you. Something big."

My pulse quickened. "What is it?"

"It's about the Navarra family," Jordan said. "You're still working on that one, right? My grip tightened on the phone, the words sinking in like a stone in my gut. This was it. The lead I had been waiting for, the one that could break the story wide open, that could expose the truth once and for all.

But then I remembered Alessandra's face, the fear in her eyes, the desperation in her voice. You can still walk away... But if you don't...

"Are you there?" Jordan asked, his voice pulling me back to the present.

"Yeah," I said, my voice distant. "I'm here."

"Good," he said. "We need to move fast. If you're in, I

can meet you tomorrow with the details. But this is risky, Steven. More than anything you've ever done."

I closed my eyes, the weight of the decision pressing down on me like a vice. The truth was right there, within my grasp. But so was the danger. The risk. The possibility that this could all end in disaster.

But in the end, I knew there was only one choice I could make. The same choice I had made all those years ago when I first picked up a pen and decided to tell the truth, no matter the cost.

"I'm in," I said finally, my voice resolute.

"Good," Jordan said, relief evident in his voice. "I'll see you tomorrow."

The call ended, and I set the phone down, staring at it for a long moment. I guess I knew what choice I was making.

Chapter 46

The Trap

Steven

I made my way through the dimly lit streets, the city's usual hum replaced by an unsettling silence. The location Jordan had given me was tucked away in a desolate part of town, far from the bustling heart of New York. A place where deals were made in the shadows, where the light of day never quite reached. It was the kind of place that swallowed secrets whole, where people disappeared without a trace.

My heart pounded in my chest, each step bringing me closer to what I believed would be the breakthrough I'd been chasing for weeks. This lead was supposed to be it—the connection that would tie everything together, the one piece of evidence that could bring the Navarra family's empire crashing down. Jordan had been clear, almost too clear, about the gravity of what he had uncovered. The gravity of what was at stake.

But as I neared the warehouse—an old, abandoned building on the outskirts of the city—a sliver of doubt crept into my mind. The location, the timing—it didn't add up. Why meet here, in the middle of the night, instead of a neutral location like we'd done before?

My instincts, honed by years of chasing stories in dangerous places, were screaming at me to turn back. I'd been in situations like this before, where the air was too still, where the shadows felt like they were closing in around you. I knew better than to ignore that gut feeling.

And yet, I kept moving.

Because even when the danger was staring me in the face, the promise of the truth was louder.

I checked the alley behind me one last time, making sure I hadn't been followed, before slipping through the side entrance of the warehouse. My fingers hovered over the phone in my pocket. One call to Nate and I could have backup. But doing that meant admitting I was in over my head. It meant acknowledging that this time, my instincts might actually be right.

I pushed forward, ignoring the warning bells in my mind. I'd come too far to walk away now.

Jordan had never steered me wrong before. I knew he had his demons, but we all did in this line of work. And I had trusted him, had followed his leads before, eventually walking away with a story that made a difference.

The warehouse loomed ahead, its rusted exterior bathed in moonlight, as I crept toward the entrance. Every instinct told me something was off, but I ignored the warning signs. I was too close to the truth to back out now.

The sharp crunch of tires on gravel stopped me dead in my tracks. I turned, heart pounding, as a sleek black car rolled up beside me, its windows tinted and reflective under the pale glow of the streetlights.

The window lowered just enough for me to see her face. Alessandra.

"Get in," she said, her voice low and urgent.

My fists clenched. "What are you doing here?"

"Saving your life," she snapped. "Now get in before it's too late."

For a moment, I considered running. But her eyes—filled with fear and something else, something I couldn't quite place—held me in place. I cursed under my breath and climbed into the passenger seat, slamming the door behind me.

Alessandra weaved through the quiet streets, her hands gripping the wheel like it was the only thing keeping her steady.

"How did you know I'd be there?" I demanded, my voice cutting through the silence.

"Because my father set you up," she admitted, her gaze fixed on the road ahead. "I overheard him talking about it earlier today. He wanted to send a message."

My jaw tightened. "And you just decided you'd send a message of your own, then? Or is this part of your father's plan?"

She flinched, her knuckles whitening around the steering wheel. "No. I wasn't supposed to be involved at all. But when I heard what they were planning, I couldn't let it happen. I couldn't let them do this to you."

"And I'm supposed to believe that?" I spat. "After everything?"

She pulled the car to a sudden stop at a red light, her head whipping around to face me. "Believe what you want, Steven. But I just saved your life. You'd likely be dead right now if I hadn't shown up."

The truth of her words hit me like a punch to the gut,

knocking the wind out of my anger. I turned away, staring out the window as the light turned green and the car began to move again. My mind was a storm of conflicting emotions —gratitude, suspicion, and something far more dangerous: longing.

The car fell silent after that, the weight of her words suffocating. I stared out the window, watching the city move past us, but my mind wasn't focused on the glowing skyline or the distant hum of life still pulsing through the streets. It was on her. On the woman sitting just inches away from me, who had somehow managed to save my life and rip it apart all at once.

I wanted to believe her. I wanted to believe that she had shown up tonight because she cared, because some part of the woman I had loved was still fighting to protect me. But trusting Alessandra wasn't something I could afford to do— not when she was the reason I had been walking into that trap in the first place.

"How far does this go, Alessandra?" My voice broke through the silence, harsher than I intended. "How long have you been keeping tabs on me? Did your father send you, or did you just go off script for this little rescue mission to clear your conscience?"

Her grip tightened on the wheel, her knuckles ghostly white. "I've always been trying to protect you, Steven. Even if you don't want to believe it. Even if it kills me."

I let out a bitter laugh. "Protecting me by lying to me. Classic."

We pulled up outside my building, and she put the car in park, her fingers lingering on the steering wheel as if letting go would break her. For a moment, neither of us moved, the only sound the steady hum of the engine. I should've gotten out. I should've walked away and left her sitting there, alone in the glow of the streetlights. But instead, I opened my mouth and said something I hadn't meant to.

"Come up."

Her head turned sharply, eyes wide with surprise. "Steven—"

"I won't ask again."

For a second, I thought she might refuse. But then, silently, she killed the engine, grabbed her bag, and followed me inside.

The elevator ride was silent. The tension between us was palpable, the air thick enough to drown in. Alessandra stood rigid next to me, her arms wrapped around herself as if trying to shield herself from whatever came next. I couldn't stop watching her, the glow of the dim lights catching the curve of her jaw, the slight tremble in her fingers.

I clenched my fists, trying to keep my thoughts straight. I should be livid that I'd been played by Mathis. But all I could think about was the fact that she was here. That she had saved me. That even after everything, my body still ached for her in a way I couldn't control.

When the elevator doors slid open, we stepped out wordlessly. My footsteps echoed down the hallway, hers just a beat behind, until we reached my door. I unlocked it, pushed it open, and stepped aside to let her in.

Alessandra walked in slowly, her eyes scanning the room like she was stepping into enemy territory. She stopped near the couch, her back to me.

I closed the door and leaned against it, arms crossed. "Why did you really do it?" I asked, my voice low but sharp. "Why save me?"

She turned to face me, her eyes flashing with something

fierce. "Because I couldn't let them kill you, Steven. I couldn't—" Her voice broke, and she quickly recovered. "I don't care what you think of me. But I wasn't going to let you die."

"And I'm supposed to trust you now?" I stepped closer, my anger boiling over. "After everything you've hidden from me, after leaving me in the dark, you think you can just show up and save the day?"

"I didn't ask for your trust," she shot back, her voice rising to match mine. "But you owe me your life, whether you like it or not."

I took another step toward her, the space between us shrinking. "What do you want from me, Alessandra? What do you really want?"

Her breath hitched, and for a moment, I thought she might slap me. But instead, she closed the distance between us, her hands fisting in my shirt as she pulled me toward her.

The kiss was explosive—fueled by anger, by pain, by everything we hadn't said. Her nails dug into my shoulders, and I responded with equal intensity, backing her against the wall as the weight of the past and the uncertainty of the future collided in a frenzy of need.

Her fingers tangled in my hair, and I groaned into her mouth, the taste of her igniting something primal inside me. There was no room for thought, no space for second-guessing. Just the heat of her body against mine, the desperation in her touch, and the way she whispered my name like a prayer.

I lifted her off the floor, her legs wrapping around my waist as I carried her toward the bedroom, the path between us a blur of kisses and desperation. Every barrier we had built to protect ourselves crumbled, leaving only raw, unfiltered need.

Tonight, though, nothing else mattered—not the threats, not the lies, not the shadows waiting for us at dawn. There was only us, clinging desperately to the little time we had left.

But tomorrow? The danger, the lies, the truth still waiting to unravel us—those things wouldn't disappear just because we wanted them to.

Still, for now, I let it be enough. I let her warmth lull me into the illusion that we could stay like this, just for a little longer. Because if tonight was all we had, I wasn't ready to let it go.

Not yet.

Part Four

Final Choices

Chapter 47

The Ultimatum

Alessandra

The humid night air clung to my skin as I slipped out of Steven's apartment, the city lights blurring in my vision as tears threatened to spill. I wiped at my eyes quickly, swallowing the sob rising in my throat. I had to keep moving. I had to leave before he woke up and saw me like this—before I did something even more reckless than what I had already done.

I hadn't meant for it to happen. I hadn't meant to lose control. But the moment he kissed me, all the walls I'd built crumbled. The weight of my father's expectations, the suffocating secrets, the danger—it all fell away in his arms. For those brief, stolen hours, I let myself believe we could exist in some other world, one where we weren't on opposite sides of an invisible war.

But that world didn't exist. It never had.

I slipped into the car, the leather seat cool beneath me and pulled the door shut. As I pulled away from Steven's building, I watched the city blur past in streaks of neon and shadow. My body still hummed from his touch, my lips still tingling from his kisses, but none of it could mask the gnawing dread inside me.

I should have known better. I did know better. I knew this would only make things worse, that I couldn't control what happened next. My father wouldn't care that I had saved Steven tonight. He wouldn't care that I loved him, that I had tried to keep him safe. My father only cared about one thing: loyalty. And I had betrayed him.

After I parked in the garage of the estate, I closed my eyes and let the memory of Steven's touch wash over me, bittersweet and fleeting. He had fallen asleep with his arms wrapped around me, his breath warm against my neck. I had watched him for what felt like hours, memorizing the way his eyelashes brushed against his cheeks, the way his chest rose and fell with each breath. Part of me had wanted to stay there forever, to forget the world outside his apartment and pretend that we were just two people in love, free of the weight of secrets and betrayal.

But I wasn't free. I never had been.

I stepped out of the car, the silence seemed to close in around me. I took a deep breath, steeling myself for whatever came next.

I hesitated for a moment, the night eerily silent, before slipping inside. The familiar creak of the old floorboards beneath my feet felt louder than ever, and I winced at the sound. My heart pounded as I moved quickly through the darkened hallways, hoping no one would see me, not even the night staff. If anyone did, they'd report back to my father, and I couldn't risk that.

When I reached the corridor leading to my father's study, I stopped, pressing my back against the wall as I tried to steady my breathing. I wasn't supposed to be here—not yet, not without being summoned. But waiting for him to call me would be like waiting for my execution. I needed to know what he was planning.

As I stood there, gathering the courage to enter, I heard my father's voice, muffled by the heavy doors but unmistakably filled with rage. "How could you let this happen? Steven Porter got away, and that is unacceptable!" The force of his anger sent a chill down my spine. "You had one job, and you failed. Do you have any idea what this could cost us?"

The man he was berating mumbled something in response, but his words were too low for me to make out. Whatever he said only seemed to anger my father further. "I don't want excuses! We can't afford mistakes like this, not with everything on the line."

I heard the sound of heavy footsteps, the man retreating under the weight of my father's fury. The door creaked open slightly as Gino exited, his face pale and drawn. He barely glanced at me as he hurried past, clearly eager to escape the storm he had just weathered.

As he disappeared down the hallway, the oppressive silence settled over the space once more. I knew I couldn't delay any longer. Taking a deep breath, I steeled myself and pushed open the door.

The room was dimly lit, the only light coming from the fire crackling in the large stone fireplace. My father stood by the window, his back to me, staring out at the sprawling estate that had been our home for generations. The faint glow of the flames highlighted his formidable figure, making his presence all the more imposing.

I took a step forward, the soft shuffle of my shoes breaking the silence. He turned, his gaze narrowing the moment he saw me.

"You're back," he said, his voice deceptively calm. But there was an edge to it—a sharpness that sliced through me like a knife.

A chill ran down my spine. Of course, he knew. My father knew everything that happened in his domain. Nothing escaped his notice, especially when it involved me.

I forced myself to meet his gaze, standing as tall as I could despite the way my knees threatened to buckle.

His eyes darkened. "I know where you've been."

Of course he did. He always knew.

"You've been with him," he continued, his voice growing colder. "Again."

I swallowed hard, the lump in my throat threatening to choke me. "Yes." There was no point in lying. He'd see through it, and it would only make things worse.

He took a step closer, his presence overwhelming, suffocating. "Do you realize the position you've put this family in, Alessandra? The danger you've brought to our doorstep by indulging in this... foolishness?"

"It wasn't foolishness," I said quietly, my voice barely above a whisper.

His gaze hardened, and for a moment, I thought he might strike me. But instead, he turned away, pacing toward the fireplace. "You've made things worse," he said, his tone flat, almost emotionless. "Steven Porter was supposed to be dealt with tonight. Instead, he's alive, and you've made sure of that."

I stepped forward, desperation clawing at my chest. "Father, please—"

"No," he snapped, spinning around to face me. "Enough. You think you've bought him time, but you've only delayed the inevitable. This ends now."

The ice in his tone sent a wave of dread crashing over

me. "What do you mean?" I asked, though deep down, I already knew.

"Steven must be eliminated," he said, his words cutting through the air like a death sentence. "And you, Alessandra, will be the one to do it."

The room seemed to tilt, the air sucked out of my lungs. "No," I breathed, shaking my head. "I can't."

"You will," my father replied, his voice devoid of any sympathy. "Or I'll send someone else. And I assure you, if I have to send someone else, his death won't be quick or painless."

Terror clawed at my throat. "Father, please—there has to be another way. I'll make him leave. I'll make sure he never comes back."

"No." He cut me off, his voice sharp as a blade. "I've given you too much leeway already, allowed you to indulge in this foolishness for far too long."

He took a step closer, his presence looming over me like a dark cloud. "Do you understand how this makes me look?" he continued, his voice low and dangerous. "How it makes you look? You want to lead this family, to earn the trust of the men, but how can they respect you when you can't even handle a single journalist? You've shown weakness, Alessandra, and weakness in this world is a death sentence."

His words cut deep, hitting on the very fears I'd been battling since I returned to the family. I had struggled to earn the trust and respect of the men who had been loyal to my father for years, and now this... this failure was a glaring reminder of how precarious my position truly was.

"Do you think they'll follow you if they see you can't control your emotions? That you let a man get too close, endangering everything this family has built?" His tone was harsh, relentless. "They'll see you as weak, incapable of making the hard decisions. They'll see you as a liability."

I stood there, torn apart by the impossible choice laid before me, knowing that no matter what I did, it would come at a cost I wasn't sure I could bear.

"The time for indulgence is over. It ends now."

The finality in his tone sent a wave of dread crashing over me. The room seemed to tilt, the floor dropping out from under me as the full weight of his words hit me.

"No," I breathed, shaking my head in disbelief.

"There is no other way," my father said, his voice like ice. "He knows too much, and he's too dangerous to be allowed to live. This is the price of your actions, Alessandra. You brought this upon the family and yourself."

Tears welled up in my eyes, but I blinked them back, refusing to let them fall. I had always known my father was ruthless, but this... this was beyond anything I had imagined. He was asking me to choose between my loyalty to the family and the man I loved. A choice that was impossible, that would destroy me no matter what I decided.

"If you refuse," my father continued, his tone unyielding, "I will consider it an act of betrayal. And you know what happens to those who betray this family."

The threat hung in the air, heavy and oppressive. I knew what he was capable of, knew that he would follow through on his word without hesitation. But the thought of killing Steven, of being the one to end his life, was more than I could bear.

"I need time," I said, my voice trembling. "I need to think."

"There is no time," my father replied coldly. "You will do this, Alessandra. And you will do it tonight."

The finality of his words caused me to shiver. There

was no escape, no way out of this nightmare. I was trapped, caught between two worlds, two loyalties that were tearing me apart.

Without another word, I stumbled out of the study, my breath coming in short, panicked gasps as I fled down the corridor. The walls seemed to close in around me, the weight of my father's ultimatum crushing me from all sides. I had always known that my life was not my own, that my choices were limited by the demands of the family. But this... this was a choice I couldn't make.

The man I loved, or the family that had shaped me into who I was. It was an impossible choice, one that would cost me everything, no matter what I decided.

When I reached the garden, I collapsed against the stone wall, gasping for air. Above me, the stars were faint and distant, barely visible through the haze of the city lights. Somewhere out there, Steven was asleep, blissfully unaware of the storm about to descend on him.

Tears streamed down my face as I pressed a hand to my chest, as if I could somehow hold the pieces of my shattered heart together. My father had given me an impossible choice: kill the man I loved or watch him die at the hands of someone who wouldn't hesitate to make him suffer.

My father had given me an ultimatum. But as I stood there, my mind reeling, I realized that I had to make a choice. I had to decide who I was willing to betray: my father, the man who had raised me and shaped me into the woman I had become, or Steven, the man I had loved and lost, the man who still held my heart.

I wiped the tears away, my hands trembling.

It was a choice that would define the rest of my life. And as I walked into the night, I knew that whatever I decided, there would be no going back.

Chapter 48

Come What May

Steven

The empty bed beside me was like a slap in the face. The sheets were cool where she had been, but her scent lingered faintly in the air—vanilla and something else uniquely her. For a moment, I just stared at the ceiling, trying to make sense of the hollow ache in my chest.

I ran a hand through my hair, cursing softly under my breath. Last night had felt like a dream—her touch, her breath, the way she had melted into me like she belonged there, like we hadn't been ripped apart by years of betrayal and secrets.

But now she was gone. Just like before.

My fingers clenched around the rumpled sheets as frustration surged through me. She hadn't left a note, hadn't awakened me to say goodbye. One moment, she'd been in my arms, and now it was like she had disappeared into thin air.

Of course, she left. Alessandra had always been good at

that—disappearing when things got too real. But this time, it was different. I wasn't that wide-eyed kid she'd walked out on all those years ago. And last night...

I sat up, my mind replaying every moment—the way she kissed me like she was starving, the way she trembled beneath my hands, the way we had lost ourselves in each other like no time had passed. But it had. Too much time. Too many lies.

And now she was gone again, without so much as a word.

I swung my legs over the side of the bed and sat there for a moment, elbows resting on my knees, head in my hands. My emotions were a tangled mess—anger, confusion, desire, and that renewed ache in my chest that wouldn't go away. Part of me wanted to be furious with her, to convince myself that she had used me again, just like before. But another part—the part that remembered the way her voice trembled when she begged me to leave, the way she clung to me like I was the only solid thing in her crumbling world—knew that wasn't the whole truth.

She was trapped, just like I was.

I got up, pacing the room as frustration and confusion twisted in my gut. What was I supposed to think? That she regretted it? That she couldn't face me in the morning? Or was this just part of the same pattern—one step forward, two steps back, always keeping me at arm's length?

The cool wooden floor grounding me as I moved through the apartment and headed for the kitchen I brewed a pot of coffee, the aroma filling the kitchen as I leaned against the counter, waiting for it to finish. My thoughts drifted back to the night before—the way her nails had dug into my shoulders, the way she whispered my name like it was both a plea and a confession. I could still feel her, taste her, as if she'd left a part of herself behind.

But she hadn't. She'd taken it all with her when she walked out the door.

I clenched my jaw and shook my head. I didn't have time for this. Not now.

Placing my mug in the sink, I made my way to the bathroom where I showered quickly, letting the cold water shock me back into focus. By the time I got dressed, I had forced Alessandra to the back of my mind. There were bigger things at stake. The investigation. The story. The truth.

Several documents were still spread across my desk, the evidence I'd been piecing together for weeks. I sank into my chair and leaned forward, scrolling through the files on my laptop. The tangled web of transactions and shell companies stared back at me, daring me to unravel it. This was the story that would break the Navarra family's hold on the city—the one that could cost me everything.

But even as I tried to lose myself in the work, my thoughts kept drifting back to her.

Why had she really come back? Why had she saved me last night, risked everything to pull me out of that trap her father had set? And why had she left like that—after everything we'd shared?

I sighed, rubbing a hand over my face. Maybe I'd never understand her, not fully. Alessandra was a contradiction—a woman torn between two worlds, between loyalty to her family and whatever was still between us. And as much as I hated to admit it, part of me still wanted to believe there was a way out for her. For both of us.

But that was dangerous thinking. Hope was a trap.

I buried myself in the work, letting the adrenaline take over. The deeper I dug, the clearer the picture became. The

Navarra family wasn't just pulling strings—they were the puppeteers behind half the corruption in the city. Politicians, law enforcement, corporate executives—they were all tied to the Navarras through a network of bribes, offshore accounts, and favors.

I stared at the documents in front of me. My hands trembled slightly, not from fear, but from the electric thrill of knowing I'd gotten this far. I had found the missing piece, the final key to unlocking the labyrinth of corruption I'd been chasing for months. And it all led back to the Navarra family.

It had taken months of careful digging, late nights flipping through stacks of paper and tracking down anonymous sources willing to talk. But the work had paid off.

It had all started as a simple lead—a tip from an inside source about suspicious wire transfers linked to a prominent New York politician. But the more I dug, the more it became clear that these transactions were just the tip of the iceberg. The real power behind it all was the Navarra family, pulling the strings from the shadows.

I leaned back in my chair, exhaling a shaky breath. The adrenaline pulsed through my veins, a potent mix of triumph and dread. I knew the power of what I had in front of me, the danger it posed not just to the Navarra family, but to me as well. Once this story was out, there would be no turning back.

I spent the next few hours verifying the information, cross-referencing it with the records I'd collected over the months. There were emails between high-level officials, bank statements showing massive, unexplained deposits, and payment orders to offshore accounts. The clock on the wall ticked relentlessly, but I paid it no mind. My focus was singular, my determination unshakable.

As I worked, the puzzle pieces began to clearly fit together: the politician's campaign funds swollen by Navarra money, the contracts awarded to businesses with ties to organized crime, and the encrypted correspondence that hinted at far darker dealings—hit orders, bribes, and blackmail. Every detail had to be airtight, every name, every transaction indisputable.

By midday, I knew had everything I needed. The story was practically writing itself in my mind, the words flowing as if they had been waiting for this moment. I opened my laptop, fingers flying across the keyboard as I began to type. This was more than just an article—it was an exposé, a bombshell that would rip through the city's power structures, leaving no one untouched.

As I wrote, my thoughts drifted to Alessandra. I wondered where she was, what she was doing, and if she knew how close I was to finishing this. Part of me hoped she would see the article before it was too late, that she would understand why I couldn't stop. But another part of me feared what her reaction might be, what she might do if she found out. Or worse, what might happen to her when her father found out she could have stopped me and didn't.

The sun had dipped below the horizon by the time I finished the draft. I sat back, staring at the screen, my heart pounding in my chest. This was it. The truth was there, in black and white, ready to be unleashed. But with it came a wave of unease, a gnawing sense that once this was out, everything would change.

I shook off the doubt, reminding myself why I was doing this. It wasn't just about the story—it was about justice, about exposing the darkness that had ruined so many lives, including my own. I had to believe that this was the right thing to do, even if it meant risking everything.

With a deep breath, I attached the draft to an email and hit send. The message zipped through cyberspace, landing in my editor's inbox with a soft *whoosh*. There was no going back now.

I sat in the silence of my apartment, the weight of what I'd just done settling over me like a thick fog. The adrenaline had faded, leaving behind a hollow ache in my chest. I wanted to believe that this would bring closure, that once the truth was out, I could finally move on. But as I stared out the window at the city lights, I couldn't shake the feeling that the hardest part was yet to come.

Alessandra's face flashed in my mind, her eyes filled with a mix of love and fear that had haunted me since seeing her so close last night. I wondered if I did see her again if it really would be the last time.

The truth was out there now, waiting to explode into the world. And with it, I knew, would come consequences—ones that I couldn't foresee. Whatever happened next, I was ready. I had to be. But as Alessandra's face lingered in my mind, I couldn't help but wonder if she was ready, too—or if she had already made her choice.

Chapter 49

An Impossible Choice

Alessandra

I hadn't slept. My heart pounded in my chest, the reality of what I was facing closing in on me. I had always known that being a part of this family meant making hard choices, but I never imagined I would be faced with something like this.

Nico was waiting for me at the bottom of the stairs, his face etched with concern. He had been with our family for as long as I could remember, a loyal retainer who had served us with unwavering loyalty. But he was more than just a servant—he was a confidant, someone who had always looked out for me, especially during the times when my father's expectations felt too heavy to bear.

"Miss Alessandra," he greeted me softly, his voice tinged with a hint of something I couldn't quite place—was it worry? Or perhaps resignation? "You look tired. Do you need to rest?"

I shook my head, too drained to argue, but something in his eyes made me pause. There was an unspoken understanding between us, a recognition of the turmoil I was trying so hard to hide.

"Nico," I said quietly, my voice barely above a whisper, "there's something I need to talk to you about."

He studied me for a moment, then nodded, gesturing for me to follow him. We walked through the grand hallways of the estate, the silence between us heavy with unspoken words. Finally, we reached a small sitting room tucked away from the main part of the house, a place where I had often sought refuge as a child when the weight of the world seemed too much.

When he closed the door behind us, the soft click sounded like a gunshot in the quiet. "You're troubled," he said simply, his tone gentle but firm. "Tell me what's on your mind."

I paced the room before finally facing him, my throat dry. I took a deep breath, trying to steady my nerves. "It's Steven," I began, my voice barely above a whisper. "My father wants him dead." The words came out fast, like ripping off a bandage, but the pain didn't ease. "He gave me an ultimatum."

Nico's expression didn't change, but I saw a flicker of something in his eyes—something that told me he already knew what I was about to say. "I see," he murmured, his voice even, calm. "And you're struggling with this choice."

I nodded, unable to meet his gaze. "I can't let anything happen to him," I whispered, my voice breaking. "But if I don't... if I don't do what my father asks, someone else will. And it will be worse—so much worse."

Nico was silent for a long moment, his eyes narrowing as he considered my words. Then, he took a step closer, his voice dropping to a low, conspiratorial tone. "There are times when difficult choices must be made—choices that shape the future, not just for yourself, but for everyone around you."

His words sent a chill down my spine, but I forced myself to listen, to understand what he was trying to tell me.

"Your father is a powerful man," Nico continued, his voice steady, measured. "But power is not absolute. There are those within the family who have grown uneasy with his methods—who believe that it's time for a change, one that doesn't rely on fear and violence."

I looked at him, the implications of his words slowly sinking in. "Are you saying..." I hesitated, my heart racing as I struggled to comprehend what he was suggesting. "Are you saying that I should... take his place?"

Nico's eyes met mine, his gaze unwavering. "I'm saying that sometimes, the only way to protect what you love is to remove the threat at its source."

His meaning struck like a thunderclap. I staggered back, my breath hitching. "You want me to challenge my father?"

The air seemed to leave the room, my breath catching in my throat as the full weight of his words hit me. Remove the threat. My father—the man who had raised me, who had shaped me into the woman I had become—was the threat. And if I wanted to protect Steven, if I wanted to save him from the nightmare that was closing in, I would have to eliminate the one person who stood in the way.

Nico stepped closer, his tone firm but gentle. "I'm saying you've already made your choice, Alessandra. You're fighting for him. For Steven. But to save him—and yourself—you may have to do the unthinkable."

My stomach twisted with revulsion. How could I even consider such a thing? My father was ruthless, yes, but he was still my father. The man who had taught me everything

I knew about survival, about power, about loyalty. How could I betray him in such a way?

But as I looked into Nico's eyes, I realized that this wasn't just about me. It was about Steven, about the lives that would be destroyed if my father continued down this path. It was about the future of the family, the future of the people who had placed their trust in me.

"I can't," I whispered, my voice trembling with the weight of my own indecision. "He's my father."

"You've seen what your father is capable of," Nico said softly. "Do you really believe he'll stop with Steven? Or will there always be another threat, another sacrifice he demands from you?"

Images flashed through my mind—my father standing over me, teaching me how to fire a gun at fifteen. The cold look in his eyes when he talked about betrayal, about loyalty. I remembered the blood on his hands. Then, I saw Steven's face last night, the way he had looked at me like I was the only reason for him to exist.

I gripped the back of a chair to steady myself.

Nico's voice remained gentle as he said, "I know this isn't easy, Signorina. But the choices we make define who we are—and who we will become. If you want to protect Steven, while ensuring that you and your family survive, you may have to make a choice that you never thought possible. You've always been stronger than you think. Make the right decision, not the easy one."

Tears welled up in my eyes, the enormity of what he was saying crashing down on me. I had been fighting this war inside myself for too long, and now the battle lines had been drawn. My father on one side. Steven on the other.

I had always known that this life required sacrifices, but

I never imagined that the greatest sacrifice of all would be my own soul.

"I need time," I said, my voice shaking as I fought to keep the tears at bay. "I need to think."

Nico nodded, his gaze understanding. "Take what time you can," he said softly. "But remember, time is not on your side. Your father will not wait."

I nodded faintly, but the words burned inside me. As I left the room, the walls of the estate seemed to close in, suffocating me.

As I walked through the empty hallways of the estate, the grandeur of my surroundings felt like a mockery, a cruel reminder of the life I had been born into—a life that had led me to this impossible choice.

When I reached my bedroom, I collapsed onto the bed, tears streaming down my face. The weight of the impossible choice crushed me.

I loved my father. But I loved Steven more. I always had. And no matter what decision I made, I would lose a part of myself.

I could still hear Steven's voice from last night—*What do you want, Alessandra?*

His eyes had been so warm, so open, like he was begging me to be honest, to fight for something real between us.

And I hadn't been able to give him a real answer.

But it was Nico's voice that echoed now, louder, stronger: Sometimes, the only way to protect what you love is to remove the threat.

I buried my face in the pillow, sobs wracking my body. What kind of person was I becoming if I could even consider killing my own father? But what kind of person would I be if I let Steven die?

I lay there for what felt like hours, my tears finally

drying on my cheeks. The moonlight cast shadows on the walls, and somewhere outside, the city buzzed on without a care for the war raging inside me.

By the time I sat up, the answer was already there, waiting for me like it had been all along. I couldn't let Steven die. No matter what it cost me.

I wiped the last of my tears away, my hands trembling.

This wasn't just a choice. It was the defining moment of my life.

Chapter 50

The Confrontation

Alessandra

The corridors of the Navarra estate felt colder than usual, the familiar grandeur of the place suddenly oppressive, as if the walls themselves could sense the storm brewing within me.

I walked slowly, each step heavy with the weight of what I was about to do. My father's study was just ahead, the door closed as always, a barrier between him and the world he controlled with an iron fist.

I paused outside, my hand hovering over the doorknob, my breath catching in my throat. I had come here so many times before, but today was different. Today, I was about to challenge the man who had shaped my entire life, who had raised me to be strong, to be ruthless.

But right now, I wasn't sure if I could be either.

I took a deep breath, pushing the door open, and stepped inside.

The scent of leather, wood polish, and cigar smoke wrapped around me like a familiar prison. My father sat behind his massive oak desk, the glow from the fireplace casting long shadows across the room. He looked up as I entered, his eyes narrowing as he registered the determination on my face.

"Alessandra." His voice was calm, but the undercurrent of displeasure was unmistakable. He gestured to the chair in front of him. "Sit."

I ignored the invitation, closing the door quietly behind me. "We need to talk, Father. About the family. About Steven."

His jaw tightened at the mention of Steven's name. "We've already discussed this. You know what must be done."

"No," I said, stepping closer to the desk. "We need to discuss alternatives."

His eyes darkened, and I could feel the storm gathering behind them. "You're being naive, Alessandra. This is the way things are done. It's the way they've always been done. Compromise is weakness, and weakness has no place in this family."

My heart sank at his words, the finality in his tone striking me like a blow. "But what if we tried something different? What if we found a way to protect the family without—"

"Enough!" he snapped, cutting me off. His fist came down hard on the desk, the sound echoing through the room like a gunshot. "You're starting to sound like your mother, God rest her soul. You think love will save you? Save this family? Love is a weakness, Alessandra. It blinds you to what's necessary. Your mother—" He stopped, as if the memory was too raw even now, but then continued, voice colder than before. "She believed in love too. It made her soft. It got her killed."

The mention of my mother sent a jolt of pain through me, memories of her soft voice, her gentle touch, flooding my mind. She had always tried to shield me from the darkness of our world, to show me that there was more to life than power and control. But in the end, it had cost her everything.

"She wasn't weak," I said, my voice hardening. "She was the strongest person I've ever known."

"And look where that strength got her," he snapped. "Buried."

I swallowed the wave of grief clawing at my throat. "Maybe you're wrong. Maybe what killed her wasn't love. Maybe it was this family's refusal to change."

He leaned back in his chair, studying me with those cold, calculating eyes that had always made me feel like a child under his scrutiny. "What future do you want, Alessandra?" he finally asked, his voice low and dangerous. "A future where we roll over and let our enemies devour us? One where we turn the other cheek and hope for mercy?"

"I want a future where we can survive without losing our humanity," I replied, my voice trembling with the intensity of my emotions. "A future where we don't have to kill the people we love to protect ourselves."

His lip curled, and the chair creaked as he leaned forward, hands clasped on the desk. "You think you can save this family with ideals? With hope? You're a fool."

I felt something inside me break at his words, the last fragile thread of hope snapping under the weight of his relentless pragmatism. "So you think that killing Steven will make me stronger? That it will make me more like you?"

His eyes bore into mine, and I saw the answer in them before he even spoke. "Yes. Because once you've done it, you'll understand. You'll see that the only thing that matters is survival. And to survive in this world, you have to be willing to sacrifice everything."

My chest tightened, the air in the room suddenly suffocating. The man who had raised me, who had shaped me into who I was, was standing before me now, asking me to destroy the one person I had ever truly loved. And in that moment, I knew that there was no turning back.

"I can't do it," I whispered, my voice barely audible. "I can't kill him, Father."

His expression hardened, a flicker of disappointment passing over his face. "Then you're not ready to lead this family. You're not ready to take on the responsibility that comes with power. You're just like her."

The accusation stung, cutting deeper than I had expected. I felt a sob rise in my throat, but I swallowed it down, forcing myself to meet his gaze. "Maybe I am like her," I said, my voice stronger now. "Maybe that's not such a bad thing."

For a long moment, we just stared at each other, the silence between us heavy with all the things that would never be said. I could see the anger in his eyes, the frustration at my defiance. But beneath it, I thought I saw something else—something that looked almost like regret.

But if it was there, it was gone in an instant, replaced by the cold, unyielding man I had always known. "You have until tonight," he said, his voice devoid of any warmth. "Kill him, or I will. And if you choose to defy me, I will make sure you regret it."

I stood there, frozen, as he turned away and walked back to his desk. My breath came in short, shallow gasps, and I could feel the tears building, but I refused to cry in front of him. Not again.

The weight of his words pressed down on me,

attempting to suffocate me, but I forced myself to keep walking, to put one foot in front of the other until I was out of his office, out of the room where so much of my life had been decided for me.

When I reached my room, I closed the door behind me, leaning against it as the tears came again. I slid down to the floor, burying my face in my hands as sobs wracked my body, the enormity of the decision I had to make was too much.

I knew that I had to choose. One life for another. One future for another. I couldn't run from it any longer.

Tonight, everything would change.

I wiped the tears from my face, forcing myself to breathe, to think. The room was silent, the darkness thick and oppressive, but my mind was racing, my thoughts spinning in a thousand different directions. The faces of the two men I loved, in such different ways, flashed through my mind, their voices echoing in my ears.

I stood slowly, feeling the heaviness of my decision settle over me like a shroud. I walked to the window, staring out at the night sky, the stars barely visible through the haze of the city lights. I pressed my hand against the glass, the cold seeping into my skin, grounding me in the reality of what I had to do.

The choice I would make.

In that moment, I didn't know which path I would take. I didn't know whose life I would save and whose I would end. All I knew was that by this time tomorrow, the world as I knew it would be irrevocably changed.

Chapter 51

The Set-Up

Steven

The city lights stretched out beneath me like a living, breathing entity, the familiar sounds comforting in its constancy. But tonight, there was no comfort to be found—not in the city, not in the glow of my laptop, not even in the culmination of months of work that lay before me. The final draft of my article sat open on the screen, every damning detail of the Navarra family's empire meticulously laid out, ready to be exposed to the world.

I should have felt triumphant. But all I felt was the gnawing sense that something was coming, something I couldn't outrun.

The soft chime of my phone broke the silence, and my heart stuttered when I saw the name on the screen. Alessandra.

For a moment, I just stared at it, torn between the urge to answer and the instinct to let it ring out. After last night—after everything—I wasn't sure what I was ready to hear.

But my thumb moved on its own, and before I could stop myself, I answered.

"Steven." Her voice was soft but urgent, like she was trying to stay calm and failing. "I need you."

I exhaled, running a hand through my hair. "You left without saying goodbye. Now you want me to drop everything and—"

"Please." The crack in her voice silenced me. "It's important. I'm sending a car."

I paused, trying to sift through the emotion weighing down her words. "Why do I feel like you're not telling me everything?"

There was a long silence, the kind that felt like it stretched across years. "Just trust me," she said finally. "I'll explain everything when you get here."

Trust her. The words echoed in my mind, hollow and uncertain. But beneath the wariness, there was something else—something that felt like hope, like a pull I couldn't resist.

"Where are you?" I asked, my voice quieter than I intended.

"I'll have the driver take you there," she said quickly, as if afraid I might change my mind. "Steven... please come."

The line went dead, leaving me standing there, phone in hand, trying to decide whether I was making the biggest mistake of my life.

The sleek black car arrived ten minutes later, the driver stepping out without a word and opening the door for me. I hesitated for a moment, staring down the dimly lit street, wondering if this was a trap or salvation—or maybe both.

The next thing I knew I was sliding into the backseat of a black sedan because she'd said she needed me.

The ride was quiet, the only sound the hum of the

engine as the city blurred past the windows. My mind was a mess, caught between memories of the woman I had loved and the reality of the danger she represented. Last night, she had been real, vulnerable, and so was I. But then she left, and now I was being pulled into something I didn't understand.

By the time the car stopped, my pulse was racing. We were on the outskirts of the city, the streetlights flickering weakly as the driver opened the door for me. I stepped out, the cool night air biting at my skin as I took in the abandoned warehouse looming before me.

I turned to the driver, but he was already back in the car, pulling away and disappearing into the night.

The warehouse door creaked as I pushed it open, the dim glow of a single overhead light casting eerie shadows across the room.

Then I saw them—two figures standing in the center of the warehouse, their faces obscured by shadows. As I approached, one of the figures stepped forward, and my heart nearly stopped.

It was Alessandra.

She was flanked by her father, Lorenzo, his imposing figure casting a long shadow over her. They were waiting for me, their expressions unreadable.

"Alessandra."

Her head snapped up, and for a moment, I thought she might cry. But then she straightened, her expression hardening. "You shouldn't have come."

"You called me," I reminded her, my voice sharper than I intended.

She looked away, her gaze falling to the floor. "I had to."

My mouth went dry, the reality of the situation crashing down on me. This was no ordinary meeting. This was a trap, one I had walked into willingly, blinded by my need for answers.

"Why am I here?" I asked, trying to keep my voice steady.

Lorenzo's cold, calculating gaze fixed on me, a slow smile spreading across his face. "You've been quite the nuisance, Mr. Porter," he said, his voice smooth as silk. "Poking your nose where it doesn't belong. But now, it's time for you to pay the price."

I glanced at Alessandra, searching her eyes for any sign of the woman I once knew, the woman I still loved despite everything. But all I saw was a mask of determination, her true emotions buried beneath layers of duty and fear.

"I'll ask again. Why am I here?" I demanded, my voice rising.

Lorenzo chuckled, the sound sending a chill down my spine. "You're here because you couldn't leave well enough alone. Because you thought you could bring down the Navarra family with a few words on a page. But you were wrong, Mr. Porter. Dead wrong."

Alessandra took a step forward, her eyes locked on mine. "Steven, please," she pleaded, her voice cracking. "Don't make this harder than it already is."

Her words cut through me like a knife, the desperation in her voice almost enough to make me reconsider. But I couldn't. I had come too far, uncovered too much. The truth was out there, waiting to be exposed, and I couldn't turn back now.

"I'm not the one making things hard," I said, my voice firm. "And regardless of what happens tonight, the world is going to know the truth about you and your family."

The silence that followed was deafening, the weight of

my words hanging in the air. Lorenzo's smile faded, replaced by a look of cold, hard resolve.

"I'm afraid this is the end of the line for you, Mr. Porter," he said, his voice a low growl.

Before I could react, the sound of a gun being cocked echoed through the warehouse, and I realized with a jolt of horror that Alessandra was the one holding it. She raised the weapon, her hands trembling, tears welling in her eyes.

"Alessandra, don't," I whispered, my heart pounding in my chest. "You don't have to do this."

She didn't respond, her finger hovering over the trigger, her entire body shaking with the weight of the decision she was about to make. I could see the conflict in her eyes, the battle between love and duty tearing her apart.

"Please," I said, taking a step closer. "If you ever loved me, don't do this."

The tears began to spill over, running down her cheeks as she struggled to maintain control. I could see her resolve crumbling, the love we once shared fighting to break through the darkness that surrounded her.

But before I could say anything else, a sharp voice cut through the tension.

"Enough," Lorenzo barked, his patience wearing thin. "Alessandra, do what you were brought here to do. End this now."

Her eyes met mine, and for a moment, the world seemed to stop. Time slowed, and in that instant, I saw the choice she was about to make—a choice that would change everything.

Chapter 52

Life-Altering Choices

The cold steel of the gun was the only thing grounding me. As I stood there, my hands trembled so violently I thought I might drop it. The weight of the weapon was nothing compared to the crushing burden on my heart. I was drowning, pulled under by a tidal wave of emotions—love, fear, duty—all colliding, leaving me paralyzed.

He'd shown up. I'd told myself he wouldn't. I'd hoped to God he wouldn't. After everything I'd put him through I assumed he'd hear my request and laugh. But here he was and now...

Steven's words echoed in my mind, slicing through the fog. *If you ever loved me, don't do this.* How could he even question that? I had loved him then, and I loved him now—more fiercely, more desperately than I had ever thought possible. But that love had led us here, to this unbearable moment where no path forward could spare us from devastation.

Behind me, my father's voice cracked through the

silence like a whip. "Do what you were brought here to do. End this now."

His command hit me like a blow, each word stripping away the defenses I had clung to my whole life. He had raised me to be strong, to be loyal, to protect the family at all costs. But now I saw the cost for what it really was.

My breathing grew ragged, tears stinging my eyes. I could feel Steven watching me, but I didn't dare meet his gaze. Not yet.

Just pull the trigger, I told myself. Just end it. But I couldn't.

"Alessandra." His voice was soft, almost tender, like he could see the battle raging inside me. He took a step closer, his movements slow, deliberate. "You don't have to do this. There's another way."

Is there?

I wanted to believe him. I wanted to take his hand and run, to leave the Navarra legacy behind, to rewrite our story with a different ending. But this world didn't allow for fairy tales. The Navarra name wasn't just a legacy—it was a curse. Blood and loyalty were its price. And the man standing behind me, my father, was the embodiment of that curse.

My fingers tightened around the gun as tears blurred my vision. I tried to summon the strength to obey, to follow through on the command that had been drilled into me since I was a child. But with each passing second, my resolve crumbled. How could I kill the man I loved when all I wanted was to save him?

I glanced back at my father. His expression was hard, unyielding—a reflection of the life he had carved out for me.

Then I turned back to Steven. His gaze locked with mine, and I saw everything I needed to know in the way he looked at me: love, forgiveness, and something deeper—acceptance.

"I'm sorry," I whispered, my voice cracking under the weight of everything I couldn't say.

Steven's eyes widened, but he didn't move. He stood there, steady, waiting. He knew.

The gun shook in my hand as I raised it. My breath came in shallow gasps, my chest tightening with every second that passed. This was it—the moment that would define everything.

I glanced at Steven one last time. Then at my father.

Forgive me.

With tears blurring my vision, I closed my eyes.

And pulled the trigger.

The gunshot exploded through the warehouse, deafening and final.

What Happens Next?

Stay tuned for part two of the Shadows Trilogy, *Shadows of Power*.

About the Author

I write romance for readers who crave a little drama, suspense, and a little simmer in their happily-ever-afters. With brooding heroes, fierce heroines, and dangerous desires, my stories explore love that burns hot—and sometimes leaves a scar. If you're looking for passion behind closed doors, you've found the right author.

I'm a southern girl at heart, fluent in sweet tea and the art of saying 'bless your heart' when the situation calls for it.

facebook.com/jcarrwrites
instagram.com/jcarrwrites
tiktok.com/@Jcarrwrites

Made in the USA
Coppell, TX
15 June 2026

81435973R00164